Bailey's Beads

Bailey's Beads

A Novel

Terry Wolverton

Faber and Faber
Boston • London

First published in the United States in 1996 by
Faber and Faber, Inc., 53 Shore Road, Winchester, MA 01890

Library of Congress Cataloging-in-Publication Data

Wolverton, Terry.
 Bailey's beads : a novel / Terry Wolverton.
  p. cm.
 ISBN 0-571-19891-0 (cloth)
 1. Mothers and daughters—United States—Fiction. 2. Lesbians—United States—
Fiction. 3. Coma—Patients—Fiction. I. Title.
PS3573.0573B35 1996
813'.54—dc20   96-14735
                                                          CIP

This is a work of fiction. Names, characters, places, organizations, and events are either products of the author's imagination or are used fictitiously. Any resemblance to actual persons, living or dead, or events is entirely coincidental. Some actual locales have been depicted for verisimilitude, but the events portrayed there are completely invented.

Jacket design by Susan Silton

Printed in the United States of America

10 9 8 7 6 5 4 3 2 1

To my mother, whose love is unwavering.

To Susan, always.

To Linda Garnets, who sheds light into dark places.

Acknowledgments

To Susan Silton for her irrepressible belief. To Robert Drake for un-yielding faith and good humor. To Betsy Uhrig for warmth, enthusiasm, and careful editing. To Valerie Cimino for picking up the reins. To Jacqueline De Angelis, Noelle Sickels, and Lynette Prucha for incisive criticism and ongoing support over many years. To the many others who provided generous and necessary feedback: Nancy Agabian, Teresa Barnett, Ann Oliver Block, Mary Casey, Ana Castanon, Sheryl Cobb, Elise D'Haene, Wendi Frisch, Sarah Jacobus, Ronna Magy, Sasha Marcus, Julia Salazar, and Robin Strober. To Bia Lowe, whose intelli-gent questions guided me to find the end. To Tom Schumacher, who *kvelled,* then rolled up his sleeves. To Liz Bremner and Brenda Funches, Linda Griego, Debra Hirshberg, Deborah Irmas, Willette Klausner, Gin-ger Lapid-Bogda, Linda Preuss, Leslie Stone, and Jeri Waxenberg, who invested in me and kept the faith. To Jeane Jacobs for sharing her own story. To Ellen Lazares for sharing the theory and the practice. To Linda Garnets for standing by. To Ginny Tal for research assistance. To Jen-nifer Cheung and Steve Nilsson, for their evocative images. To the Cal-ifornia Arts Council, whose support kept me going. To the Los Angeles Gay and Lesbian Community Services Center, for its commitment to art and to artists. To my students, an unending source of inspiration. To Anne Benvenuti, whose own writing first suggested to me that a splin-ter can pierce the heart.

During a solar eclipse, just before that radiant orb is totally obscured, tiny specks of light glitter at its edge, forming the appearance of a string of beads around the dark disc of the moon. These lights are known as "Bailey's beads," after the astronomer who first observed them, the last brightness visible in the darkening sky.

1.

Bryn

*I can hear
the ticking of my heart,
round, full notes
resonant and clear
as an old grandfather clock
housed in a case of solid oak,
polished and smooth
to the finger's touch.
It's a sound
as slow and ancient
as time itself,
this careful, measured beat
from the drum of the world.
A sound
that seems to emanate
outside of me,
as though the heart
had fled
the prison of my chest,
or as though I,
this consciousness,
this sense of self,
had been evicted
from the body,
while the heart still keeps time.*

2.

Djuna

With an absent curiosity she regarded the hands that guided the steering wheel, their ghostlike color in the zinc gray light, their unfamiliar contours. Disembodied hands, not connected to herself. It was someone else who was driving the car as her eyes drilled through the windshield into the sweep of night. Someone else who decided when to turn, where to aim the headlights. The feet on the pedals were disembodied too, and subject to conflicting impulses, one foot leaning on the accelerator, urging the car forward, *faster, hurry*, while the other pressed the brake as if in an act of prayer, desperate to stop, willing the hands to throw the shift into reverse, the wheels to retrace their path homeward, commanding time to roll back to the way things were before.

"Before" could be any moment prior to the one when she'd plucked up the receiver. She'd been fearless then, not knowing there was anything to fear; this gesture held no terror, this simple act committed dozens of times each day: the phone rings and you answer.

She'd expected a client, a friend, a salesman on the other end of the line, expected anything at all except the unknown voice with its incomprehensible message. The words were already fragmenting by the time they reached her ear, shards her brain struggled to piece together into something that made sense.

Her lover.

An accident.

The hospital.

Come.

Djuna Rifkin, a former journalist, an inveterate seeker of information, for once had found herself empty of questions, except for one that formed itself not in her brain but erupted from the back of her throat: *How bad is it?*

Later she would remember other fragments of her conversation with the cop: *Her car was struck on the passenger side by a panel truck; witnesses say the guy changed lanes without any warning, totally his fault; he was pronounced dead at the scene; your friend was taken, unconscious, to the emergency room at Cedars-Sinai. Your name was in her wallet to contact in an emergency.* Later she would play and replay the graveled sound of his practiced neutrality, the details of his story, but for now she could only recall the break in his voice, the crack in his control as he answered her sole question: *It doesn't look good. I'd get over there pretty quick if I were you.*

Someone had heeded his advice. Someone was driving the car, dodging the slow-going motorists, the hapless left-turners, but Djuna watched it all from a distance, sealed inside a thick, transparent membrane wherein time moved on a different track than that of the frantic, charging car.

While that someone maneuvered her way onto the freeway entrance ramp, Djuna was thinking about a certain kind of argument she always had with Bryn, frequent enough to be played out in shorthand, a few words summarizing the points they had so long debated. "The will," was all Bryn had to say, and Djuna would look up, shamefaced and defensive.

"I know," she would reply, her own annotation of the myriad reasons and excuses that composed her inaction. How she could not bring herself to make a will because she was convinced that, once it was signed and witnessed, she would die. How her fear of death was paralyzing.

"It's not fair," Bryn would sometimes continue, if her frustration loomed larger than the containment of shorthand. "God forbid, if something should happen to you, your family could just waltz in here, take everything that belonged to you, and slam the door in my face. Is that what you want to happen?"

It hadn't happened, Djuna thought now, as the car merged from one freeway to the next in seamless choreography, becoming one more streak in the stream of taillights snaking west. *This* had happened, and although she did not yet know all the ramifications of *this*, already, in her mind, it had assumed the proportions of disaster, momentous and irretrievable.

"I'll just have to make sure I die first," Bryn had sometimes threatened, but Djuna could tell that even Bryn realized she was being overly dramatic. Still she would persist, "At least that way, *you'll* be taken care of, and I won't have to suffer the indignity of being left out in the cold."

It was during one of these discussions that Bryn had announced that she'd begun carrying a slip of paper in her wallet: In case of emergency contact Djuna Rifkin. She'd wanted to make certain it was Djuna who would be in charge, and not Bryn's family. She made Djuna promise that she too would carry a card in her wallet, with Bryn's name printed in the blank, but, Djuna realized guiltily, she had never gotten around to that either.

Djuna gazed dully through the windshield, trying to determine where she was. The car seemed to have an intelligence all its own; it knew which exit to take, to go straight through the first stoplight and turn right at the next. Often she and Bryn would skirmish over directions, Bryn headstrong and insistent, commanding, "Go *that* way," but Djuna could always pull rank. Djuna had lived her entire life in Los Angeles; she knew every shortcut, the peak traffic hours, the less-traveled cross-town routes, as if her own veins and arteries were a road map of city streets. Tonight, though, the city loomed beyond the glass, ominous and unfamiliar, devoid of recognizable landmarks. It was only the car that knew where to go, and for this, Djuna was grateful.

She'd always told Bryn that she couldn't die first, because Djuna would never be able to cope with the grief of losing her, of staying on alone. Bryn was stronger, Djuna was convinced, Bryn would find someone else. Before Bryn, Djuna's life had seemed as flat and mono-chromatic as a black-and-white photograph; Bryn had given it color and texture, dimension and spark. Without Bryn, Djuna feared, the spell would be broken, and her life would shrink back to a surface of two dimensions, its hues pallid, its radiance dimmed.

Fuck you, you can't die! The words slapped against her ear before she knew her lips had formed them. Their sound punctured the membrane that had shielded her, spilling her back into the car like honey swirled from a spoon, and, part liquid still, she quivered behind the wheel in the driver's seat. Her eyes caught the speedometer, glowing white in the dark car; the red needle showed that she was doing fifty-five, perhaps not the sanest speed on La Cienega Boulevard.

Bryn was a snappish, impatient driver who kept up a running stream of invective against her fellow motorists: "Let's go, let's go, would you get a fucking *move on?*" She was highly skilled and disciplined at the wheel, though; rarely did she do anything reckless or stupid, and she always wore a seat belt. She hated being a passenger, was always tense when someone else was driving, even Djuna. As a child Bryn had lived with a stepfather who drove like a terrorist, holding his family hostage while he sped down the freeway in the wrong direction, cackling at the oncoming drivers who swerved, dumbfounded, to avoid him.

Djuna had never met the man; he'd divorced Vera, Bryn's mother, years earlier, and had disappeared from Bryn's life like a tornado funneling toward the horizon, indifferent to the wreckage left in its wake. There was so much of Bryn's life Djuna only knew from stories—the city she'd grown up in, the years she'd spent as an actress on the stage, how she'd been an alcoholic—stories Bryn had lived without her, pieces of Bryn she could never fully know.

Not like Djuna, whose life was like a constant river flowing through the city of the angels. The hospital where she was born. Every school she'd attended. Her family and friends, her ex-lovers, all still dotted the landscape of everyday life. The past might be past, but that was no guarantee she wouldn't run into it standing in line at the movies.

It was the presence of Bryn in her life, four years now, that helped Djuna demarcate the past and present, Bryn who made it possible to say, "Once I was that kind of person, but now I am like this. Now I am loved." This, most of all, was the gift that Bryn had brought her, the knowledge that she, Djuna Rifkin, was loved and therefore worthy of love. It was like the first kiss of sunshine on her skin after spending her life in a cave underground.

The car seemed to have lost its ability to pilot itself; as she approached Third Street, Djuna remembered at the last minute that she needed to turn there and jerked the car into the left-hand lane while brakes squealed and a horn blared behind her. Once she reached the hospital complex she circled the block three times, not because she didn't know where she was going, but to delay the shuddering ascent into the concrete parking garage.

On her third pass by the Beverly Center shopping complex, she recalled the voice of the cop, urgency severing its professional calm: *I'd get over there pretty quick if I were you.* Fear washed in her belly like water through a sieve. Djuna longed to push away the implication of those words, to press the accelerator and speed far from this place, head for the ocean, not stop until she reached its hem. Instead she pulled into the garage, wound up and up and up until she found an open slot, and left her car.

Under the blinking fluorescents, stripped of the armor of her automobile, Djuna heard the lonesome clack of her boot heels as she crossed the concrete floor. The chilled night air raised gooseflesh on her arms; she hadn't thought to bring a coat. Bryn was always the one to remind her: *dress warmly; put a sweater on; don't you want to take a jacket?*

Djuna stepped into the elevator and pressed a button. One restless hand brushed at the spikes of her short, dark hair. The motion of time slowed, as though she were in a dream; this was just the kind of dream she would have, too, trapped in an elevator that continued to inch upward at a torturous crawl and never seemed to arrive. Each breath she drew was sharp and shallow, a cold blade in her lungs; underneath the whine of the elevator, her ears pulsed with a drumbeat of fear.

3.

Bryn

Underwater music
swells
like the chimes
of a thousand lights.

I never learned
to swim;
I feared the depths,
the moment of suspension,
the encompassing
caress of liquid,
its ubiquity.
Once submersed,
you are in its grasp;
the law of water
is a total law,
and you surrender,
relinquish breath,
lungs shriveling to sponge.

I never learned
to swim,
but here I move
to underwater music,
an echo of lights,
a languid timbre,
the notes drawn out,
a music
of endless ripples,
undulations
of the blue-green sun.

4.

Djuna

Therapy.
The dentist.
The gym.
A class.
Two writing dates.
Three clients.
A deadline.
Another class.
Acupuncture.
A phone date.
A reading.

Djuna sat at Bryn's cluttered desk in the home they shared. Bryn's life was strewn open around Djuna, a series of splayed notebooks and folios: her date book, address book, Rolodex, "to do" list, her pad of phone messages, a sheaf of manila file folders. Bryn was the busiest person Djuna had ever known, her days and nights pared into slivers, parceled out among myriad interests and activities like a cell endlessly dividing.

While Djuna usually had a general idea of what her lover was up to, she preferred to remain aloof from the grueling details. Now Bryn's precise, angular handwriting blurred before her eyes, the sheer logistics threatening to sink her, send her plummeting beneath the surface of Bryn's teeming schedule and not let her up for air.

Each notation represented someone who expected Bryn to appear at the appointed time. That confidence was well placed; Bryn was faithful to her responsibilities. If she was late on a project, she would forgo sleep to finish it; if she was sick, she'd pack a thermos of tea, a wad of tissues, and a shopping bag of herbal remedies and continue on with her agenda. "Fanatic," Djuna had sometimes charged during futile attempts to dissuade her. "Stubborn, stubborn, stubborn."

When she'd arrived at the hospital, Djuna had half expected to find Bryn sitting up, arguing with the nurses, "I can't stay here, I'm late for my writers' group," insisting that they provide an ice pack for her throbbing head and call a taxi. Djuna had imagined Bryn contesting her medication, "There's no way I'm going to take Tylenol Three—my acupuncturist says it's bad for my liver. If you'll just hand me my purse, I've got some Rescue Remedy." But Bryn had not been sitting up exerting her will; she had in fact lain still, not moving, not speaking, eyes closed, while the doctors probed, the nurses injected, the machines assumed her bodily functions.

Tomorrow Bryn would not be keeping her commitments; already tonight she had failed to appear at the scheduled meeting of her writers' group, and the urgent blinking of the answering machine signaled the confusion of those who'd been expecting her. Wednesday, Thursday, Friday—the calendar was full of people counting on Bryn, secure in the fidelity of her promise. They would all have to be called: the clients, the students, the editors, the therapist, the dentist, the trainer, the acupuncturist. And not only them. Bryn's friends, Djuna's friends, Djuna's clients—a universe of people. And of course, Vera.

Someone was going to have to pick up the phone and dial, over and over again; someone was going to have to find the words to translate the pictures that now lurched and swooped in Djuna's head like crazed, frightened crows, their caws ferocious and mournful.

Those diving pictures. In one she was yelling at a flat-faced woman who perched behind a desk; the nurse's caramel skin was yellowed by the white uniform she wore like armor. The woman was insisting that only next of kin would be allowed into intensive care. Bryn had always warned about this: *You'll be lying there hurt, and I won't even be allowed in the hospital room.* She had drawn up legal papers, granting Djuna her power of attorney, but those documents were at home, nestled in the file drawer next to Bryn's will, unremembered until now.

The sky dropped, the picture shifted. Djuna had located a gay nurse on duty; she recalled how his face had crinkled in sympathy as she explained her plight and he'd arranged to bend the rules for her. *This hospital's pretty good about that; not all of them are. We'll honor that*

9

piece of paper, but you're gonna have to go see the hospital administrator with it. It may not hurt to have your lawyer call too.

Then she had gained admittance to a room so white it made her eyes ache even to remember. Overexposed. White walls, white curtains, white sheets, the brutal sheen of the fluorescent lights, the bandages circling her lover's skull. If ever there'd been color in the room it had been bleached away. Bryn's long gold hair hacked off at clumsy angles, the cut, bruised face, raw and mottled with veins like marble. One of the hands was not bandaged, and Djuna recalled how she'd reached to touch it, picking her way through the forest of tubes that linked Bryn to the machines surrounding the bed like steely guardians, protective and menacing. The skin of the hand was cold against Djuna's fingers, cold as the chilled, chemical air, cold as the white glint of the diamond Bryn wore on her third finger, a ring that had belonged to Djuna's grandmother.

She'd only been allowed ten minutes in the room, ten minutes and no privacy, a constant influx of doctors and nurses, a swarm of observers gawking through the plate glass window. She'd wanted to talk to Bryn, to sing, to scream, to find just the right incantation to woo her, the perfect spell to bring her back, but as each second died on the cold white face of the clock, the words sputtered in her throat and drowned. In the end, she could do no more than clutch the hand that wore her grandmother's ring and whisper, "Pie, I love you so much," before she was ushered from the room.

She'd passed a tense hour in the waiting area before she'd seen a doctor. A nurse had taken Bryn's medical history, or what little of it Djuna was able to provide. To her the questions seemed off-center or beside the point, not at all important to the essence of Bryn.

When the doctor did appear he was hurried and distracted; his eyes never once met hers. He'd been reluctant to talk to Djuna, but she'd again explained the power of attorney, that Bryn did not want her biological family making decisions about her. Remembering the advice of the nurse who'd helped her, she underscored that her attorney would be calling the hospital administrator in the morning.

After all that, the doctor hadn't known much, could only recite from the pages of Bryn's chart: *Unconscious upon arrival in emergency; aside from cuts and abrasions her major injury appears to be head trauma sustained in a car accident; she's in a deep coma and so far is not responding to any stimuli. We're running tests to determine the extent of brain damage; in the meantime we're respirating her and intravenously feeding and hydrating her. It's too early to make a prognosis, but these cases are very tricky; there's a lot that can go wrong. I can tell you this: the longer she stays under, the worse her chances.* Through it all his face remained as blank as a clean white plate.

A cat leapt onto Djuna's lap, scattering the contents of one of the folders, chasing away the pictures and the grim echo of the doctor's words. It was Toulouse, the lame tabby Bryn had adopted as a kitten years before she'd met Djuna. The cat stared into Djuna's face; his amber eyes posed questions for which she had no answers.

"I don't know when she's coming home," she said to Toulouse, who appeared to listen gravely. *Or if,* her brain amended, but her mouth refused the words. She reached out then and swept the cat into a fierce embrace, face pressed into his furry neck. The creature squirmed and struggled free, limping toward the kitchen and his empty supper dish.

Djuna plucked up the folder that was labeled Will and Power of Attorney. She held it as she might the carcass of a lizard or a rat killed in the yard by Toulouse, handling it gingerly, keeping it as far from her body as her arms could reach. From this remove she scanned the documents inside: last will and testament, living will, nomination of conservator of estate, durable general power of attorney, durable power of attorney for health care. Bryn had tried on several occasions to sit her down and explain these things to her, but Djuna could never keep it in her head. Her fingers snatched the last set of papers and then, after hesitating, also grabbed the living will. She spared no time in returning the folder to the file cabinet, closing the drawer with a resounding clang. She found Bryn's thoroughness awesome; she could not imagine another woman of Bryn's age—just forty her last birthday—so prepared for demise.

That accomplished, Djuna regarded the remaining pages strewn before her with restless disinterest. Now that she was home, she was convinced that she should have stayed at the hospital, although the entire time she'd been there she'd been stricken with an overwhelming longing to be home. No place was right. Where she belonged was with Bryn, but Bryn was missing; Djuna could find her neither in the white bed that housed the vacant stranger who wore the ring she'd given Bryn, nor in the empty rooms of their house, surrounded by the trappings of Bryn's life.

Bryn's heaped, untidy desk sat before a window that overlooked the garden, the garden Bryn had planned and tended, the flowers she'd coaxed from the ground. Beyond the glass Djuna could see nothing but fog and darkness; still, she tried to let herself imagine what Bryn saw from this view: the lemon trees dripping golden gems, the bright bloom of the hibiscus, neighborhood cats curled along the drive like punctuation marks.

Djuna's gaze returned to the papers spread before her. She would never be able to make these calls, never be able to form the words to say what she had seen, what was now true, or might be. Maybe she could ask someone to help her, to make the calls for her, but she would have to make at least one. Well, two. She would have to call Vera; she couldn't expect anyone else to call Bryn's mother.

She decided to start with Emily. Emily, who was perhaps Bryn's closest friend, was stalwart and practical, the best person to call on in an emergency. Also, she lived in the neighborhood, a few blocks away; somehow that seemed appropriate to begin with those at the closest proximity and then radiate outward, the news traveling like ripples in a pond.

The truth was that Djuna telephoned Emily at least as often as Bryn did, but because Emily had first been a friend of Bryn's, Djuna had never bothered to memorize her phone number. "What's Emily's number?" she would call out time and time again, and Bryn would dutifully repeat it, almost managing to suppress the bite of impatience in her voice.

Now Djuna beseeched, "What's Emily's number?" but the silence echoed like a yawning mouth, ready to swallow her whole. She thumbed the pages of Bryn's address book, located the listing for Emily Gresham, then needed to look it up again when her brain went as blank as the dark window before her. Reading aloud from the book, one number at a time, Djuna began to dial.

5.

Vera

A mother spends her whole life worrying that something bad will happen to her child. When Brenda was just a baby I used to lie awake at night, straining my ears to listen for the sound of her breathing, and if I couldn't hear that tiny rush of air in the dark quiet of the house, I'd get up and go in to check on her. Sometimes I'd do that three, four times a night, especially when she was really young. I was twenty years old, a new mother, and dumb as I could be, scared to death that I would do it all wrong, make some mistake that would take her away from me.

After I divorced her father—she was still just a little thing, barely a year old—I had to go to work. I left her with my mother, and I was lucky, I suppose, that it wasn't with some stranger, but still I worried all day long about the kinds of things that could happen to her with me not there to watch. Would she get up into the medicine cabinet and swallow something she wasn't supposed to? Would she wander out into the street when her grandma's back was turned?

The more they grow up, the harder it is: first they go off to school and then they want to go places with their friends and then one day it seems like they want to be anywhere except at home. You can't be there to check up on them or remind them to be careful. Kids don't understand how much it hurts to watch them and be afraid for them and know there's nothing you can do.

I remember one day, Brenda must have been about sixteen and she wanted to do something, go to a rock concert or somewhere with a boy, I don't know exactly what, but I thought she was too young and I said no. She turned around and snapped at me—she actually bared her teeth like a vicious dog—and said, "Mother, it's *my* life!" What she couldn't see was that it was *my* life too. Her life belongs to me in a way that can't ever be undone, no matter if she changes her name or moves out to California or becomes a . . . homosexual.

When you give birth, it's like God gives you a gift, but it's not for-ever, so you spend your whole life guarding it, jealous, always afraid that someone will come along and snatch it. I remember when Brenda was in grade school, there was a little boy, one of her classmates, who got run over by a car on his way home from school. The whole neigh-borhood turned out for the funeral, and of course, we all felt just ter-rible for his poor mother. She looked like that car had run over her instead, only she was still walking around. After the service, I went up to that poor woman and I took her hand and gave her my condolences, but a part of me—and may God forgive me, because I know it's evil—a part of me felt *smug*, just crowed inside like some proud rooster, be-cause *my child* was still alive, *my child* was safe.

As if I had anything to do with it, as if that wasn't the Devil himself taking credit for the Lord's work. Yet I felt like I *did* have something to do with it, the way I was always on the lookout for any danger—the strange man lurking around the school yard, the poisoned candy in the Halloween bag—always trying to keep my girl from harm. Every night I prayed for her—I still do—as though my whispered words to God could weave a secret net around her and keep her safe.

But it seemed like safety was the last thing Brenda wanted. I swear, if something was the least bit risky or even downright dangerous—whether it was the scariest ride at the carnival or the one boy in black leather with a scar on his cheek and trouble in his eyes—then *that* would be the thing that would draw her, like a moth to the porch light. She'd sneak around, go behind my back, even lie outright to my face. She probably thinks I don't know about all that, but I do; if that girl made up her mind to do something, then she was going to do it, and if it kept me up at night getting gray hairs over it, well, that was my problem.

When she first moved out to California—that was a long time ago now, almost twenty years—I thought I'd go crazy. California seemed like the most dangerous place of all. Charles Manson, Hell's Angels, all those nuts. She went out there all by herself and with practically noth-ing, no savings, no job, hadn't even lined up a place to stay. It didn't make any sense to me. She didn't know a solitary soul in Los Angeles. I never could understand why someone would move so far away from home to a place where they had no friends or family.

She was never much of a letter writer, and she hardly ever came home, once every three or four years maybe and then it was only for a couple of days. She told me one time that a couple of days was all she could stand! We always tried to make her feel welcome, and Everett would go out of his way to take her anywhere she wanted to eat, and believe me, it wasn't always easy with her vegetarian diet and all her finicky tastes. Not every man would have put up with it.

I spent years worrying myself sick about all the things that could happen to her out there, and then one day I just gave up. I thought to myself, maybe her life doesn't belong to me anymore; maybe God took back his gift after all. Or maybe I tried to hold on to it so tight that it slipped away from me. Like trying to hold on to water with a clenched fist.

So when I got the call, it was like I'd been expecting it all my life, or else like it'd already come years before. I don't mean to sound cold, or to say it doesn't hurt me like the deepest pain. It's just that I've been losing my daughter almost since the day she was born.

This is just one more layer of it. Maybe it's the final one. Or maybe not. It's like that with losing someone you love: Right when you think that every single thing's been taken from you, it always seems like there's one more thing to lose.

6.

Djuna

Inhaling the fumes of jet fuel that clogged the sky above the airport, Djuna remembered something Bryn had once said about her mother: *If the whole world were being blown up in a nuclear firestorm, Vera would find a way to make it seem like her own personal tragedy.* Vera's conversation seemed to bear that out—what a good mother she'd been, how hard she'd always tried to protect Bryn—a self-congratulatory riff tinged with the requisite whine of martyrdom that set Djuna's teeth on edge. Gripping the steering wheel, she had to fight the impulse to shriek, *Oh yeah? Well, if you were so concerned about your daughter, how come you let her grow up with a man who molested her from the time she was eight years old?* She had a longing to rip the veil of denial from this woman's eyes, to shred her pathetic fiction into little bits and cast them at her feet.

She couldn't, of course, now least of all. Setting her mouth in a grim line of self-control, Djuna maneuvered the car through the maze of autos stacked at curbside, past weary passengers loading their reclaimed baggage into trunks and back seats, aiming her wheels at the sign that proclaimed Airport Exit. On the seat beside her, Vera Collins fished for something in the recesses of her vinyl pocketbook, retrieving a puff of tissue, a wadded gum wrapper, a mirror that caught the painful glint of the sun. The air in the car was laden with her unfamiliar perfume, vaguely citrus and sharp as a slap. Its persistent odor made Djuna long for the scent of jasmine and honeysuckle that always surrounded Bryn, rising like a spell from her skin.

The airport exit ramp spit them out onto Century Boulevard, a street lined with chunky office buildings and faceless, squat hotels, billboards sprouting like weeds in a desolate field, a landscape devoid of charm. Overhead the sky was split by jets departing for unknown destinations or heading home again.

Twice before, Djuna had spent time with Bryn's mother: once on a visit to Detroit with Bryn, and then again when Vera had stayed with them in L.A. two years ago. On both occasions, Djuna had bristled with a tension like static electricity, had circled the woman warily, fearing the friction, the spark struck at the point of contact.

There had been, over the four years, exchanges of Christmas gifts, cards at birthdays, infrequent conversations on the phone, tinny with false gaiety. Their relationship was unfailingly cordial, though perhaps not warm. Vera's warmth, Djuna had always suspected, was reserved for Lowell, to whom Bryn sometimes referred as "my first wife," Djuna being the second. Unlike Djuna, Lowell was older than Bryn and endowed with inherited wealth. Djuna was convinced that, in Vera's eyes at least, Lowell was forever the more suitable partner: the loss of her lamented, someone who would have taken care of Bryn.

Djuna swung the car onto the entrance to the San Diego Freeway. A layer of ochre haze hung on the horizon, obliterating the mountains to the north. She knew she ought to be making conversation, helping to put Vera at ease, but all her words felt booby-trapped, wired and timed to explode.

She recalled Bryn telling her a story about Vera's first trip to California, not long after Bryn had moved here. Bryn had retrieved her mother from the airport and driven her straight to the beach. "You won't feel like you're in California," she'd admonished Vera, "until you see the ocean." Djuna could imagine a younger Bryn against the backdrop of the Pacific, hair gleaming in the sun as she coaxed her mother farther down the shore. The vision melted as the sign loomed for the Santa Monica Freeway; Djuna spurned its westward option, turned her back on the ocean, veering to the east.

The day was warm, too warm for the season, alleged to be winter. Vera had discarded her thick coat, now folded tidily atop her suitcase in the trunk. After a lifetime of sunny days, eyes stung by the bleached-out sky, Djuna craved the gloom and the variety of seasons. *Only because you've never experienced them,* Bryn always insisted. It was the kind of day Bryn thrilled to, reveled in, lifting her face to the sun, crowing, *Eighty degrees in February! This is why we live in California!*

Djuna pressed the switch to lower the windows, courting a breeze to blast away the heat and Vera's citrus scent, but as air gusted into the car, Vera clasped her hands around her head, protective of her hairdo, and Djuna once more slid the window shut. Her heart knocked like a gnarled fist against the hollow door of her chest; she had seen this gesture hundreds of times before, Bryn's hands fending off the wind.

"I'm sorry," Vera explained, "I just don't know when I'll get to go to the beauty shop again." Her tone was cloying, half defensive, half apologetic. She offered an anxious glance in the direction of the speedometer, disguising it by pretending to study the scenery. It was a strategy that Bryn herself had often used.

Djuna adjusted her own window to gape a mere inch; she was finding it difficult to breathe. She nosed the car to the right, into the next lane, keeping her gaze trained on the rearview mirror, the panorama of cars behind her, pressing forward. At Robertson, she exited.

"Would you like to check into your hotel first, or do you want to go straight to the hospital?" Djuna offered without inflection as she once more headed north.

"My hotel . . ." Vera flushed in confusion. "I thought I'd . . . be staying with you." Disappointment—or was it hurt—clung to her voice like a child to its mother's hem.

Djuna had prepared herself for this, armed herself against it. "Don't worry about the money," she reassured Vera, deliberately misinterpreting her distress. "I'll take care of it. Our house is pretty far from the hospital, but the hotel is just a block away. I thought it would be easier for you—I know you don't want to drive in L.A."

So calm, so reasonable. She did a credible job of sounding helpful, concerned only with what was best for Vera. The truth was, Djuna didn't think she could bear to be alone in the house with her. Without Bryn to mediate, Djuna would never be able to keep up the veneer of politeness, the aura of caretaking.

The sight of Vera's trembling lip was bad enough, but into Djuna's mind rose an image of Bryn's face, stiff with disapproval, eyes round and mournful. Bryn would expect her to take Vera in. If the situation were reversed, Djuna knew, Bryn would have gone to any lengths for Djuna's mother, Rose, for whom Bryn had a genuine affection. Djuna wished with all her heart that the situation *were* reversed; she was convinced that Bryn would handle every detail with aplomb, a generosity of spirit Djuna could not seem to muster. *I'm sorry,* she said silently, as if in prayer, addressing Bryn's stricken eyes, *I just can't do it; I'm not you.*

To Vera she said, "You'll be able to walk to the hospital anytime you want. You won't have to wait around for me to drive you back and forth."

A new concern broke like day over Vera's drawn face. At one time Vera Collins had been a beauty, but life had drained her buoyancy, leaving her body too thin, her features pinched and bitter. "You won't be there?" she inquired, the question edged with reprimand.

Djuna fought the surge of guilt that spread like a stain along her spine. "I thought we could take turns," she explained, hoping her words didn't sound as lame to Vera as they did to her. "I've got a business; I have to work, and I figured you'd want time to yourself too."

Djuna swallowed hard. Last night on the phone she had tried to dissuade Vera from coming at all, "There's nothing we can do until they know more," but Vera would not be deterred.

"I'll have Everett drive me to the airport as soon as it's light and take the first flight I can get on. I'll call you as soon as I know my arrival time.

"I need to be there in case . . . something happens. Besides, if she's unconscious, they'll need me to sign things."

Damn it, Bryn, Djuna had thought then, *you took care of drawing up all those papers but you didn't bother to tell your mother. You left that job for me.*

Now something like granite edged its way into Vera's voice, something Djuna had never heard there before. "I plan to stay with my daughter around the clock," Vera announced, and let it hang there like a challenge. *This is my commitment,* it seemed to say, *a mother's pledge; what could you possibly offer up to match it?*

7.

Vera

All day she sat beside the high metal bed in the room that was stark white. She took a certain comfort in its austerity, a cocoon in which to wrap herself, a whiteness that obliterated shadow. Vera sat in a straight-backed chair, her body taut, stiff and armored, as though it were bound in gauze, white gauze, layer upon layer, or as if her skin had grown a cottony film to hold itself intact. She held herself apart, remote and separate from the doctors and nurses—they too were clad in white—who came and went with such hurried purpose, checking the monitors, replacing the IV drip, emptying the catheter bag. She listened for their shoes, the shush and occasional squeak of the nurses' soft soles, the more blatant, self-important clack of the doctors' polished wingtips. Despite her layers of protection, the sounds got through, seeping through the gauze, penetrating the white cocoon; some part of her was being worn away—a slow and gradual erasure—by the click and hum of the monitors, their cold, impersonal music, and the sinister hiss of machines that measured what remained of her daughter's life.

Her daughter. Sometimes Vera had to struggle to retain that sense of connection to the sightless body in the bed. Not Brenda, but "Bryn," someone who had lived apart from her for nearly twenty years in California. Someone who lived with a woman as though they were husband and wife. Someone who had hired a lawyer to draw up documents just to ensure that Vera have no say in her affairs. Someone whose face was blank as the white walls, whose hands were curling into claws, someone who most likely did not even know that Vera was there, keeping watch.

Still, Vera sat by the bed of this stranger, touched her with the soothing caresses she'd bestowed on her daughter as a little girl, stroking the down of her cheek, tracing the curved shell of her ear. She helped the shift nurse to bathe the dormant body, assisted in its turning every few hours. She recut the golden hair, trying to even out the hatchet job they'd done in the emergency room, and washed it gently, drying each lock with a towel.

Had her daughter been conscious, Vera could have never done these things; ever since the age of eight or nine, Brenda had been physically withdrawn from her, from Chet, her stepfather, too, refusing kisses, shunning hugs. Had her daughter been conscious, she would have shaken her head just enough to dislodge Vera's fingers, moving beyond the reach of Vera's touch.

Sometimes Vera would clasp one of Brenda's gnarled hands and press, and every nerve in her body would jolt when she felt the hand squeeze back. "Reflex," the nurse insisted, stamping out hope the way one would smash a roach, but Vera would not be convinced.

The room contained a single window; beyond the glass loomed an impossibly bright day. All her life Vera had loved the sun, but now she kept the curtains drawn; even the sheen of light that crept between the breach offended her. The traffic noise that rose up from the street was an affront—a stab of music from a passing radio, the insult of a car alarm—reminding her that the world went on while Brenda lay here, stopped.

Djuna came every day, always in the evening, once the glow from the window had dulled, then darkened to a flat black square of night. She made polite, desultory conversation about her work, described whatever she had photographed that day. She talked about the friends who'd called with their condolences; Vera never recognized the names.

Djuna would ask how the day had gone, if Vera were comfortable at her hotel. Djuna roamed the space of the small room, shoulders hunched, gestures nervous. She aggressively questioned the nurses: "What *are* those medications?" "What *is* that you're feeding her?" "Don't you think you're being a little rough with her?" She sat on the side of Bryn's bed, her back to Vera, and ran her hands along Bryn's body with a proprietary air that Vera found sickening. Before an hour had passed, Djuna's eyes would sidle toward the door, as if she were plotting her escape.

Vera judged her harshly for her absence, her apparent lack of devotion; how could Brenda ever think that anyone would care for her better than her mother? Still, she was secretly grateful, relieved to pass the hours of waiting on her own, without the restless presence of her daughter's . . . friend. In the white room, time had slowed; Djuna brought with her speed and impatience, a sense of the outside that did not belong. Vera's days had assumed a shape, a rhythm, a pulse of waiting.

When Brenda was a child, seven or eight, just after Vera married Chet and they moved to the house in Dearborn, she took to hiding for hours at a time. Vera would come home from work and Brenda would have disappeared, although she did not seem to have left the house. In the beginning, Vera had called and searched, Chet had shouted threats to every corner of their tiny home, but they could never find her, never coax her from her covert place. Eventually, they'd given up, resigned to wait until the girl appeared. Late at night, Vera would return to Brenda's room and find her curled on the bed, munching crackers from a secret stash, a book spread open in her hands. No punishment, no beating ever yielded up her hiding place, and none could make her stop the practice.

Vera wondered to this day where she had gone; was there a corner of the basement overlooked, a high shelf in a crowded closet? Surely, after all these years, Brenda could reveal to her that secret. It seemed important, suddenly, to know, but there was no one to ask now. Her daughter was hiding somewhere inside the pale stranger on the bed, and there was nothing for Vera to do but wait until Brenda decided to return.

8.

Djuna

Sunday, February 7

The fluorescent lights of the supermarket were much too bright, and the lilt of the Muzak seemed mocking and sinister as Djuna pushed her cart through the deserted aisles. The piped-in sound delivered a wretched imitation of Al Hirt in a staccato trumpet version of an old Carpenters song, "Rainy Days and Mondays."

It was a rendition that would have made Bryn gleeful with contempt, and Djuna felt the ache of missing the wicked gleam that would spark in Bryn's eyes as she paused to listen to the song's tortured notes. She might have asked, rhetorically, "Do you think it's good marketing for the grocery store to feature a song by a woman who died of anorexia?"

It was Bryn who had gotten them into the habit of shopping after midnight. Their forays had started as an antidote to insomnia, but had become one of Bryn's favorite rituals. She liked, she said, "the opportunity to appreciate the supermarket as artifact, as a cultural phenomenon," most easily accomplished, apparently, when the store was not so crowded. "And besides," she would add, "wouldn't you rather stand in the checkout line behind a hooker than behind a housewife any day?"

Tonight, Djuna could not have said what drew her to this place; she had driven into the lot without ever planning to. Now she was staring at produce, perfectly symmetrical stacks of oranges, apples, pears, lemons, their colors impossibly vivid.

Her brain was deviled with questions. They buzzed in her cerebrum like hornets from a violated nest, swarming and stinging, releasing their poison into soft, defenseless tissue. There was no way to drive them out, no way to quell their relentless probing.

Some of the questions she had hurled like pipe bombs into the bland faces of the doctors: "What are you doing to her? Why isn't she getting any better?" She had acted tough and brash—mortifying Vera, who treated everybody at the hospital with great deference, as though they were angry gods who needed to be appeased, as though, if she were only nice enough, they'd allow her daughter to get well—but privately Djuna saw herself as small and helpless against the inscrutable doctors and their arsenal of technology. She wanted them to feel her sting, but the doctors never lost their maddening professional calm; their answers remained impenetrable, shadowed and circumscribed. All she really wanted to know was when Bryn would return, *when* not *if;* all she really wanted was reassurance. But the doctors did not speak the language of hope. Their words were instruments, precise and sterile; they told her nothing, but left her riddled with sharp incisions of fear.

Djuna didn't trust these doctors; they knew nothing of Bryn. Bryn had no faith in *any* doctor, believed that Western medicine was crude and ignorant. Bryn trusted her Chinese herbs, the gleaming acupuncture needles, slender as thread, and her own intuition about the body. Bryn would be incensed to find herself like this, strapped to a hospital bed, hooked up to machines, at the mercy of indifferent men.

What would Bryn want me to do? This question jabbed at Djuna's conscience, which was tender and swollen with guilt, because the answer was almost certainly *not* what she was doing. Djuna could still remember their fight, it must have been nearly two years ago, when, in the wake of an abnormal Pap smear, Bryn had refused to submit to the recommended surgery. They had been in the car, driving home from the appointment, and Djuna had swerved abruptly toward the curb and stopped the car.

"You *have* to have that surgery," Djuna had pleaded. "You could *die.*"

Bryn had removed her sunglasses, stared directly into Djuna's eyes. "I'll either heal myself, *my way*," she'd insisted with chilling determination, "or I'll die." She added a shrug to demonstrate her lack of preference for one outcome or another.

For Djuna, death was the ultimate fear, but Bryn seemed to find it preferable to any number of alternatives. They had that difference between them. Nothing Djuna could say would persuade Bryn to change her mind. "It's *my* life," she had maintained with a ferocity Djuna could not palliate. Either the test had been wrong or Bryn's herbal potions had proved effective: subsequent Pap smears had revealed no abnormalities.

Djuna forced her consciousness to return to the grocery store, where she still dawdled before mounds of produce. Bryn would never buy fruits and vegetables at this kind of market; she would accept only organic produce. Frequently on their late-night jaunts, she would bemoan the passing of the all-night health food store where, years ago, she and Lowell used to haunt the midnight aisles.

What would she think about the tube that carried nourishment from her nose to her stomach, and what did they put in that tube? Bryn, who was always so strict with her diet, had a litany of foods she would not eat: meat *and* chicken, coffee, sugar, chocolate, eggs, butter, oils, ice cream, anything with preservatives. And of course, alcohol and drugs.

If Bryn could decide for herself, would she take the medication that the nurses injected several times a day? Djuna knew the answer was no. Bryn never took drugs, not even aspirin; she was an addict, she would always explain, she could not medicate. But she also believed in the power of the body to heal itself; drugs, she was certain, would only impede that process, weakening the body, its defenses. Again and again she tried to sway Djuna to this wisdom, implore her to shun antibiotics for the flu, eschew painkillers for menstrual cramps. Djuna wanted to believe, but her faith was not that strong. When her symptoms worsened, she would run to the doctor for a prescription, while Bryn sadly shook her head.

Djuna had a persistent fantasy that Bryn's continued coma was a way of protesting her hospital confinement: "I'm not coming back until you get me out of here." Djuna imagined bringing Bryn home, tucking her between her favorite green flannel sheets in her own bed, *their* bed. Toulouse would come and sit atop her chest, monitor the beating of her heart with his own. Djuna could sit beside her all day and stroke her skin, something she was less than comfortable doing under Vera's disapproving scrutiny.

As easily as she could picture this, as much as she knew Bryn would have preferred it, the scenario collapsed when she tried to imagine announcing to the doctors that she was taking Bryn home. They would argue, their words hacking away at her resolve; Vera would be horrified, who knew what she would do? Djuna had no doubt that if the situation were reversed, Bryn could have pulled it off, defying everybody, taking matters into her own hands; she had that much faith. This was another difference between them. *What if I'm unfit to be the guardian of Bryn's life?*

Djuna found her cart making a right turn; this was an aisle they would have ordinarily ignored but she browsed it with studied concentration, as though she'd developed a sudden fascination with cookware. Muffin tins, omelet pans, basters, and measuring cups; the careful stacks had a soothing effect.

Still, they could not drown the buzzing in her ears. There were other questions too, each a slippery rung on a ladder of fear she climbed and descended and climbed again in fitful dreams that she could not escape by awakening. She knew that Vera judged her heartless and disinterested because she picked up her camera and went to work instead of sitting at Bryn's side each day. *How else am I supposed to get money?* Djuna bitterly queried a rack of coffee mugs.

At least Bryn had health insurance. She'd gotten a policy for catastrophic coverage just last year, after more than a decade of having none; *had she been prescient?* Still, there were copayments that would undoubtedly add up to thousands of dollars. *How am I going to manage to pay the mortgage? What am I supposed to do about the bills that keep arriving?* Every day they stacked higher on Bryn's cluttered desk.

Bryn had not only bestowed on Djuna the responsibility for her medical care, but a general power of attorney as well. Thus, Djuna was empowered to conduct Bryn's affairs, to sign her checks, to make decisions. *But what are the right decisions? Should I act as if this is a temporary crisis, a momentary disruption, as if, in a week or two, Bryn will wake up and resume her life?* If Djuna had been the type to pray, this is what she would have prayed for. *Or is this the end of everything familiar? Should I be liquidating Bryn's retirement account, paying off her debts, putting the house up for sale?*

Each shuddering step down the ladder brought her closer to the unimaginable: the end of her life with Bryn. She could not will herself toward that conclusion, so she allowed herself to hang, suspended in space, poised on an upper rung, unable to take the next step.

A chill traveled the back of her neck. She was in the frozen-food section, staring into frost-filled bins of boxed vegetables, Lean Cuisines. In the bottom of her cart lay three tins of Band-Aids; she could not remember how they had gotten there. With an effort at purposefulness, she wheeled the cart around, rolled it back to the aisle labeled Personal Care and replaced the Band-Aids on the shelf. She tossed a container of dental floss into the cart, then put it back.

There were also the questions Djuna could not bring herself to ask, queries that rose on the lips of friends who did not seem to realize that their words, so innocently released, fell like hammers on her heart. They were questions about Bryn: *What was her mental state? Had she been unhappy lately? Do you think it could have been . . . deliberate?*

People seemed to take comfort in believing that every action was intentional; there could be no accidents, no random episodes that erupted without warning, shattered the foundations that held you. People told themselves these stories to reweave the illusion of control whenever it threatened to fray: a sick person would get well if only they'd resolve their inner conflicts; a rape victim must have somehow "asked for it." Thus, if Bryn had had an accident, she must have unconsciously wanted to hurt herself.

It was common knowledge that Bryn had in the past attempted suicide; her poem "Lament of the Failed Suicide," had been published in a number of anthologies, and she'd written about the seductive allure of death in three of her short stories. There had been at least two episodes, once as a teenager and then again in her twenties. Razor blades the first time, pills the next. "The second time, it almost worked," Bryn had said.

Sometimes Bryn still struggled with despair. Djuna always thought of it as a giant hand, reaching out from Bryn's past to grab hold of her; she was certain that nothing in her present could produce those feelings. While in its grip, Bryn might gasp, "I want to die," but Djuna never bought it, or at least did not fear Bryn would take action. The Bryn that lived in Djuna's mind was indistinguishable from the love Djuna had for her, and so Djuna reasoned, "She couldn't really want to die, not when I love her so much."

But since the accident she'd had to wonder if her view of Bryn held a shred of resemblance to the way Bryn saw herself. In the weeks before the crash, Djuna had been preoccupied, caught up with her own troubles: a client who'd refused to pay his bill, the image that eluded her in her own artwork, a battle with her mother on the telephone.

When Emily had asked her, "Has Bryn been depressed lately?" Djuna hadn't known the answer.

What do I really know of Bryn? Do I even have a clue about how she feels inside? Of all the tormenting questions, these were the worst. They not only presaged a precarious future, but threatened to obliterate the past. And they made her feel so lonesome.

As if to taunt her, the Muzak began a lugubrious string version of Gilbert O. Sullivan's, "Alone Again, Naturally." A song about suicide. If Bryn were here, she would have sung along, exaggerating the theatrics of the histrionic tune. She knew all the words to almost every song, the trashier the better. She would have made Djuna laugh and banished all her questions.

But Bryn was not here. Djuna suddenly could not fathom what she was doing in the grocery store. There was no reason to shop, no one to shop for. Abandoning her empty cart, she turned abruptly and escaped the store, stomping her way through the electronic doors, heading for the parking lot, where the halogen lamps cast an eerie illumination that robbed the color from the night.

9.

Bryn

Under the red light,
everything is
feverish;
images swim
into being,
up through their
chemical bath,
like early life forms
spawning
in primordial soup.
Images swim,
but the pictures
don't quite form,
remain elusive,
out of focus;
lines and shadows
won't assemble into
recognizable shapes,
into anything like meaning.
Instead,
they swirl like vapor
across the surface
of a white screen,
collecting,
darkening,
menacing.
Sometimes
they almost resemble
something I might
once have known;
then they
dissolve again,

their promise
unfulfilled.
The shapes
come and go,
like ominous clouds,
but always,
the red light burns.

10.

Djuna

Nights, she spent in the darkroom, coaxing pictures from strips of film, manipulating shadow and light. It was the best time of the day, when she could be alone in the cool quiet, under the glow of the red light, where everything looked ghostly, not quite real. It was better than lying rigid, sleepless, in the bed grown suddenly too wide, better than staring into the radium grin of the clock, while each minute rolled interminably into the next. In the darkroom she could lose herself in work, rid her brain of everything but contrast, texture, the quality of light.

During the daytime it was different. Her life assumed a distorted shape of normalcy: she answered her telephone; held meetings with prospective clients; went out on photo sessions, arranging her lights, her tripods, an array of props. Point. Focus. Shoot. All of it required interaction, demanded that she *be* someone, pull herself up from the ocean floor where she had sunk, marooned, that she break the surface of the water, breathe the unfamiliar air her lungs were dead to.

It was too much for her. With Bryn absent (and that is how Djuna thought of it—*absent*—as though her lover were on a long trip, some remote place with no telephones, no postal service, but from which she was certain to return), Djuna's carefully nurtured self seemed to have vanished, a protective wrapping peeled away, dissolved, as if in acid. Now everyone could read her like an X ray.

Easiest were the clients who knew nothing about her: the bored musicians, the high-strung art directors nursing ulcers; they expected nothing more from her than her function, and she obliged. Others, though, had crossed the border in quasi friendship; they knew about Bryn's accident, inquired about her status, and watched with anxious eyes for any sign of lagging competence in Djuna. They found none, her style edgy and stark as ever, unsettling, brutal.

With friends it was more difficult; they had a stake in Bryn's recovery that competed with her own. Djuna fended off their questions, deflected their attempts at solace; she could no more accommodate their grief than she could bear to deal with her own. Many friends were clamoring to visit Bryn, but Vera was opposed to visitors and Djuna did not override her. Emily called every day with a new report; she was spending her lunch hours at the library conducting research on comas, and trumpeted her latest finds to Djuna in lengthy faxes from her office. Emily took comfort in facts—recovery ratios after six months of coma, strategies of rehabilitation from head injury, length of survival in cases of persistent vegetative state—but Djuna could scarcely stand to look at them.

As always, the worst people to contend with were the members of her own family. Djuna's mother, Rose, had a real affection for Bryn, but still could do no more than murmur empty words of comfort: "Oh honey, don't worry, I'm sure it's going to be all right." On the other hand, Sid Rifkin, Djuna's father, continued to display a remarkable talent for making her feel worse: "It's all well and good that she makes you responsible for everything. That hospital bill could be tens of thousands of dollars; I suppose you're gonna be responsible for that too?"

Good old Sid—Djuna felt the bitter taste of metal in her mouth—always holding the value of a dollar above all else. As a child, she had longed to be an artist, an aspiration quickly snuffed by her immigrant father, who only wanted for his children financial security. He had traveled to this country as a young man, fleeing the horrors of Europe in the 1930s, and built his furniture store from nothing. There was never any question that the Rifkin children would join the family business; from the age of seven Djuna had gone to work after school and on weekends and all summer long, filing orders, counting inventory, carrying deposits to the bank, tasks that left her seething with boredom. She learned to hate the smell of wood, the sharp aromas of polishes and stains, the scratchy nub of upholstery against her fingers.

Her decision, at age twenty-four, to leave behind the opportunities at Rifkin's Fine Furnishings had been momentous; she was still the only one of her siblings to have done so. After spending a few years as a freelance journalist, she had finally sought another world through a camera lens. Rejecting her father's plan for her had been perhaps more transgressive than declaring herself a lesbian; it was not until she'd become successful that her father had forgiven her.

Commercial photography had handed her a livable compromise: a modicum of creativity and a respectable, if not lavish, income. She'd developed an apocalyptic style: buildings undergoing demolition, crumbling façades, broken glass and splintered boards, the smoking aftermath of fire were among her signature backdrops. It was a sensibility untypically female, and it had earned her a reputation on both coasts. She'd assumed she was content.

It was Bryn who'd pushed her into making art, Bryn who'd glimpsed another vision lurking just beneath the slick and brittle surfaces of magazine ads and album covers, Bryn who'd given voice to what Djuna had barely dared to dream.

The print Djuna pulled from the developer was a desert scene in black and white, the earth cracked from the sun's heat, a lone saguaro standing like a sentinel, the sky a vast terrain stretched beyond the borders of the photograph. Just below the line of the horizon appeared the image of a spinning figure, only partially burned in, incomplete and mostly blurred, yet delicate and slight in a way that suggested female. Her wheeling limbs were indistinct, her face unformed; she appeared to have been caught midway, dissolving into or out of the landscape.

This belonged to a series Djuna called "Disappearing Angels," on which she'd been working since the fall. In May she was supposed to have an exhibition of the series, her third solo show in the two years she'd been making art, but she couldn't allow herself to think even that far into the future, not right now. All she could do was breathe in the sour fumes of chemicals, trace her finger over the still-wet surface of the page. She couldn't make out much in the dim illumination of the red bulb, but she didn't want it any brighter than that; she found some distant consolation in the dull ache of the crimson light. Frowning, she speared the photo with a pushpin through its thin white border, adding to a line of photos on the stucco wall.

When she'd first begun to do her own work, departing from what Bryn disparaged as "the eighties sensibility" of her commercial shots, Djuna had found herself drawn by the elemental, taking pictures of flame, rock, trees, fog. The human figure was entirely absent, although she portrayed matter with a sentience her strutting rock musicians could only covet. It had been in the last nine months or so that bodies had begun appearing in her photographs, though never quite corporeal, instead as phantoms, wraiths, half-realized, evanescent beings, tenuous in the solid landscape.

Bryn had her own theories about this gradual genesis, and she'd spin them for hours, late into the night, sitting up with Djuna while she printed in the darkroom. Bryn never seemed to need to sleep, and made no complaint about the late-night hours; in truth, she loved this time, burning with the same creative fuel as Djuna, the spark passed back and forth between them. Bryn presided over Djuna's art-making process with a proprietary air, injecting her opinions whether they had been solicited or not.

Often they would spend whole nights like this, as the sky outside changed unnoticed from charcoal to pearl and the moon rose and set: bundled up in sweaters in the unheated studio, Bryn wrapped in a blanket, seated on the floor while Djuna bent over her tray of solvents, sharing a thermos of peppermint tea, spectral in the gleam of the red light.

11.

Vera

Monday, February 8

Alone amid the florid decoration of her hotel room, Vera felt time drag like a rusted tailpipe, abrasive and combustible. The room remained austere, unwelcoming, despite its air of fussy exuberance; the slick surface of the bedspread sloughed against her skin, the pillows buoyant despite the pressure of her head. The time she spent here was like serving out a sentence, each moment measured, the minutes counted, another day past.

Djuna had provided her a stack of books, favorites, she'd asserted, of Bryn's, but Vera could not manage to concentrate on any of them. They seemed barren and plotless, depressing; their alphabets coiled and squirmed before her eyes, assuming strange, unreadable shapes. The television was a more reliable companion, and the hotel was wired for cable, a luxury she did not have at home. Still, after hours of staring at the flickering images, a furtive emptiness yowled from within. Clicking off the remote in disgust, she would sit then, stunned by the silence.

Sometimes she thought of Everett, pictured him at home in their living room, parked in his customary chair, the vinyl-covered lounger he'd brought with him from his previous marriage. She could see the rhythmic dipping of his hand into a bowl of mixed nuts from which he'd first picked all the cashews—his favorite—the fingers crusted with oil and salt. Twice since she'd been here she'd telephoned him, in the evenings upon returning from the hospital to the confines of this room; she would have done it more often except that Everett frowned on long-distance calling, considered it extravagant, a waste.

Seated in a silk-covered chair, its back too low for comfort, Vera leaned against a rising edge of panic. She tried to think of all the people who might pull her from the desolation of this night: her mother, dead now for eighteen years; Everett, his mouth gritty with nut meat, fretting while the telephone bill ballooned; Brenda, beyond the reach of any telephone. The list abruptly ended there, and again Vera teetered at the brink of a fearsome void. What had happened to her life that in all the world there were just three people to whom she might look for comfort, and none of them likely to provide it?

Actually, there was one more. No sooner did the thought find a receptive niche in her brain than a surge of longing swelled in her. She wanted, more than anything in the world, to talk to Chet. Her ex-husband. Her second husband. In spite of all that had happened, she still liked him best of the three men she had married. No one could make her laugh the way Chet did, laugh like the whole world could go to hell, and in spite of everything, she missed him.

Even to her own mind, it seemed perverse. There was no question Everett was a better man; he never got drunk, didn't run around, never hit her. But he never made her laugh. Not like Chet. And he wasn't someone she could call up in the middle of the night, someone who could make her feel better, the way sipping an ice-cold martini used to make her feel better.

These were things she dared admit to no one. Even if she could have talked to them, the other three people on her list would have never understood: her mother, Everett, Brenda.

Brenda claimed that Chet had done something terrible to her; Vera's mind could not keep hold of exactly what it was, but it made her feel sad, made her feel split in two. When Brenda talked about her stepfather, her eyes grew steely, unforgiving. It made Vera sad and guilty, as though somehow she were to blame.

Sometimes Chet still called her on the phone, once or twice a year, but, as Vera explained each time to Everett, she couldn't help that. *Never could predict when that man would take a notion to do something crazy.* She always took those phone calls with an air of resignation, keeping her voice flat and uninflected, dropping monosyllables like bread crumbs on the path of his exaggerated stories. She never let him know the way her pulse would quicken, pink rising to her cheeks, or how one hand would start a slow journey along the curve of her own hip.

If Chet picked up the phone to call her, there was nothing she could do. For her to call him, though, would be another story, something she had chosen, something dangerous; the mere idea left her flushed with shame and slightly breathless.

So Vera did those things she knew to do to pass the time: twisting her coifed hair into pin curls, wrapping the whole construction in layers of toilet paper wound around her head and clipped in place, plucking her eyebrows, filing her nails and applying a new coat of polish, gliding cream into the ridges under her eyes. She performed these rituals like spells against the heaviness of time, these night hours that hung like suspended weights from thin and fraying rope.

It was so much better at the hospital, where her vigil had a quality of timelessness, where her purpose was clear and it was not necessary to think of how to occupy herself. She stayed at Brenda's bedside as much as she could, rising early in the morning, often before the sun, walking the blocks to the hospital along still-empty streets. At night she lingered there as late as she felt safe to do so. She'd even inquired of one of the nurses about the possibility of installing a cot inside her daughter's room. That way she could stay around the clock with Brenda; that way she'd never have to return to this room, this cold and ostentatious cell.

12.

Bryn

I am pursued
by blankets,
flattened squares
of darkness
advancing
through the air
in horizontal columns,
shadow planes.
They hunt me.
I want to run,
but have no body,
sheer intention
trapped
in formlessness.
No matter
how slowly
they approach,
I am slower;
I never will be
swift enough.
They mean to
capture me,
pin and hold me
with their
spectral weight,
a woolly suffocation.
I long to
get away
but they come closer,
silent and gradual

as snow;
in another moment,
I'll be swaddled.
One gasp
and I succumb.

13.

Djuna

I asked for a dream, but nothing came, my sleep as empty as the stretch of sky on a starless, moonless night. An L.A. sky, full of haze and the drone of helicopters. One lousy, stinking dream was all I asked, but the universe says, "Fuck you, you get nothing."

I thought a dream might be the way to reach you, a place where we might dare to meet; no one else would have to know. I can't believe you'd leave me so alone, without a word or sign.

Remember how you used to leave me love notes in my date book? I never knew when I would turn the page and find a message scribbled in your hand: "Today I send you kisses," or "Don't forget that you are loved." I could never figure out when you had written them. Last night I flipped through every page—March, April, May, on through to December—to see if by some chance you'd left a message there. Pie, I wanted to set that book on fire when I was done; what good is a calendar that you don't write in? What use is a year if you're not here with me?

Tonight I had to make your mother leave, after days of hoping she would take the fucking hint, me pacing around the room like a mental patient, trying to will her toward the door. But no, she's treating *me* like the intruder, the uninvited guest.

Tonight I came right out and told her, "I need to have some time alone with her"—*her,* as if you weren't even in the room. I said, as politely as I could, "Do you think you could please find something to do for a couple of hours," and of course she looked wounded, and put on her martyr's voice when she said, "I suppose I can, if you need me out of the way." But I mean, Jesus, it's been a week, and she's had you every minute!

Sometimes I think she's trying to wait me out; she thinks I'll lose interest, fade away, and then she'll have you to herself. It makes me so pissed off. If I were your husband, she could never get away with it. I found out she even asked the nurse if she could move a cot into your room and stay with you all the time! When they told me I said, "Absolutely not." If anyone is going to spend the night with you, it should be me.

Eight days, baby, since I last spent the night with you. I can't stop thinking about the last time, just last Monday night, a million years ago: the way you cried into your pillow and I lay there, stiff, pretending not to hear. I don't know why I was so goddamn stubborn. I didn't even hold you while we slept; I turned my face to the wall and let the whole night pass, listening to you breathe. I should have wrapped my arms around you, licked the tears from your face. I never imagined that I might not have another chance.

I've played and replayed that fight in my head. I keep hearing what you said to me: *I mean no more to you than the furniture! When you want to sit on the couch, you just sit; you don't ask how the couch feels or whether it likes its placement in the room. As long as you're comfortable, you just assume that everything else is.*

You thought I wasn't listening, but I was. And I got defensive, the way I do when I feel criticized. I should have said, "Without you, there's no furniture, no home at all, only a dank cave devoid of light and comfort." I didn't say that. Instead I fought back like a cornered animal, tried to make it seem like your fault. I was afraid that if you were dissatisfied you'd leave me. Is that what you've done? Is this my punishment? Oh, girl, I need another chance.

Emily says we're doing this all wrong. She threatened that if we don't start allowing visitors she's going to dress up like a nurse and sneak in to see you! She's been doing a huge amount of research—you know how she loves to research! She told me we should be talking to you all the time; she found studies that show a person in a coma can still *hear*. In one way, I hope it's true: I want you to hear me, to know how much I want you back. But on the other hand, I worry; if you can hear Vera then maybe you'll never come back. Like how, sometimes, you'll avoid her call, pretending not to be home when her voice comes over the answering machine.

It's Emily's opinion that you need a lot of visitors; if it were up to her she'd stage "This Is Your Life" right here in the hospital room. She says your brain needs constant stimulation; I say, what else is new? She told me I should bring in a boom box so you can listen to your favorite music. She thinks that even if some brain cells were destroyed in the accident, other cells can be trained to pick up the slack.

Jesus, I can't bear to think of anything wrong with your beautiful brain. How many times have you said to me, "When my mind goes, just shoot me?"

My own theory is this: It's not your brain that's the trouble, it's not that you *can't* come back, it's that you *won't*. I think you must have been scared or hurt someplace way deep inside of you, and you won't come out again until you're sure it's safe.

When I tell that to the doctors, even to Emily, they look at me in this pitying way, like "Hoo boy, this one's in *big* denial!" The only person who seems to think it's plausible is Suyuan, who wants me to get her in here to work on you. I know you'd like that, to get some acupuncture, to be in the care of someone who you trust; it's just trying to convince the doctors. *And* Vera.

Pie, my days roll by like some stupid, endless train. I return my calls, I keep appointments, I take pictures. At night I print until my eyes ache, then I fall into bed and pray for a dream. If it were me, I'd find some way to come to you, I swear.

Do you remember how we used to look up at the sky at night and fantasize about a spaceship landing in our yard? I always said I'd go in a minute if the aliens invited me, and you swore you never would. But now you have; it feels like you've gone off without me, into some galaxy I can't find with my telescope, let alone reach. You're out there, somewhere, orbiting, and all that's left for me to do is look up at that blank sky, starless night, and howl for a moon that's disappeared.

14.

Bryn

They have plucked
a thread of my skin
and begun to knit;
their needles twist
the skein of my flesh.
I am unwinding.
They are knitting
a heavy blanket
to keep the orphans
warm in winter.
Each stitch takes more of me;
I am grateful
to be of use.

The needles click
as they dance;
a pattern unfolds.
The colors are beautiful,
my bones gleam,
my veins like bright ribbon,
the spun strands
of my hair.
The room hums with gossip,
the music of old women,
their expert fingers
knotting the wool
of my flesh.
Outside, children howl
in the gathering twilight,
the orphans,

out in the cold.
I call to them:
don't worry,
it won't be long.
My shape is changing.
I will be ready soon.

15.

Djuna

Wednesday, February 10

The small office had first been decorated in the 1970s and never redone since. Cheap wood paneling adorned two walls and made the space seem even smaller than its sparse square footage. The other two walls were a neutral bisque, repainted every three years, always the same shade—Djuna had inquired. Beaded macramé holders suspended potted ferns and philodendron before the window where the miniblinds were always drawn tight. The only light in the room came from two nondescript lamps, their lampshades beige. Each rested on an identical low end table, knockoff versions of Swedish modern.

There were two chairs in the room, upholstered in the same brown wide-wale corduroy as the couch, its cushions sagging from the weight of accumulated misery. The chairs faced each other as if in discourse across the narrow width of the room, the couch lining a third wall, the silent observer. Above the couch hung a poster—Djuna recalled how it seemed like every lesbian had owned one of these in the seventies—of watercolor flowers, their petals exaggerated so as to suggest female genitalia.

Glaring at the pile of the tan carpet, Djuna reflected for perhaps the hundredth time on the ugliness of this environment, its utter lack of style or charm. It depressed her to think of Evelyn, her therapist, spending her days in this room, week upon week, confined to her corduroy chair, deprived, like the plants, of natural light. Did Djuna really expect to receive help from the person whose sensibilities this room reflected?

"What's going on?" Evelyn leaned forward in her chair, eyes fixed with that look Djuna had come to think of as "the Discerning Gaze." It was the look Evelyn would get when she was trying to read you, to figure out what secrets you might be keeping from yourself.

"I was just thinking about how much I hate this office." They had talked about this on numerous occasions in the three years she'd been seeing Evelyn for weekly therapy.

Each time, Evelyn would adopt a bright, curious expression. "Tell me why," she would urge, as if nothing made her happier than to hear that her clients thought she had execrable taste in interior design.

Today, though, Djuna didn't bite. "We've been there," she muttered, scowling, and slumped a little deeper in her chair.

"How do you feel right now?" Evelyn tried again.

The glance Djuna returned to her was shot with poison. "I feel fine, just swell," she sneered. She stole a surreptitious peek at her watch, hoping that the hour, so recently begun, might have somehow miraculously elapsed. It had not; forty of the fifty minutes remained. She fidgeted under Evelyn's expectant stare.

"So how about *you,* how do *you* feel?" Djuna knew she was being childish, bratty and obstinate; she knew, too, that she could never hope to win with these tactics.

Evelyn was quiet for a long moment before responding. Dr. Evelyn Meyer was a large woman, possessed of a maddening calm; there was about her none of the skittish self-consciousness by which some big women betray their wish to be smaller. Her curly hair was clipped short, tidy about the face; her high, clear forehead appeared to house a great intelligence.

Finally she spoke, her voice low, still clinging to a trace of a Jersey accent. "How *I* feel," Evelyn said, her eyes holding Djuna's gaze, "is very sad for you. I can see how much pain you're in, and how much rage. I just wish that you felt safe enough to let it out here."

Djuna's stomach flipped over, as if her center of gravity had been turned upside down. The skin on her face flared hot and then, just as suddenly, cold.

"Rage?" she echoed, but her voice cracked and the word broke into two disjointed syllables. Through that opening, as if a dam had ruptured, her anger began to pour. It surged through her body like a river of lava, molten and glowing, hissing steam. Before it carried her away, she had a thought, more frightening than the fever in her veins: the origin of this flaming current was not the doctors, was not Vera, was not the insensitive friends or her own oblivious family. It wasn't even Evelyn, who might have been seen to have struck the spark. It was

Bryn. Bryn, who had gone away, abandoned her completely; now only the shell of the body remained behind to taunt her. Bryn, who had heaped upon her impossible responsibilities but left no guidance, and no clue.

An image leapt before her eyes: She was shaking Bryn's inert body like a rag doll, pummeling its lax muscles like a scrimmage dummy. "Wake up, wake up," she saw herself screaming in time to the slaps that made the doll's head roll from side to side.

Djuna felt herself drowning; the burning river pulled her under, closing off breath. She stared, wide-eyed and helpless, at Evelyn, who instructed, "Tell me."

"I can't," Djuna managed to choke.

"Why not?" Evelyn was straining forward, as if her very focus was a lifeline to pull Djuna back to land.

The room seemed to darken and waver in Djuna's vision; her throat was on fire. The words came slowly, tortured, disconnected from each other, spit, smoldering, from between blistered lips: "If I . . . got . . . mad at . . . her . . . it . . . could . . . kill . . . her."

Even in this halting elocution, something was released; hot tears leaked onto her cheeks, and sobs like little hiccups emanated from her solar plexus. Once begun, she could not stop; her body rocked as she wept, and her cries escalated into howls, fierce and plaintive as a beast whose mate has been caught in a trap.

Evelyn watched for a few moments, then she did something she had never done before: She rose from her chair and in three heavy steps was standing next to Djuna. Her looming presence was at first over-whelming, making Djuna feel dwarfed and pathetic, but then Evelyn knelt down beside the brown chair and rested one large hand on Djuna's back.

She smelled of corned beef and mustard, what she must have had for lunch, but Djuna did not find it unpleasant. It made her think of her grandfather Itzak, Rose's father, the only member of her family by whom she had ever felt loved. For a moment she sat still, feeling the warmth of Evelyn's hand between her shoulders and breathing the fumes of her grandfather's deli, a smell with all the poignancy of childhood.

16.

Vera

Vera thought it was a bad idea, a gross invasion of her daughter's privacy, like being watched in sleep while you drool or snore or your nightgown rides up over your hips. Vera was certain Brenda would have felt the same; she had said to Djuna, "Would *you* want to be looked at by a bunch of strangers?" but Djuna had completely disregarded her opinion, saying, "They're not strangers, they're her friends." As if *she* knew Brenda's mind better than the mother who'd raised her from a baby. In the end, those years of sacrifice and worry counted for nothing; Djuna had the power to make the rules, and Brenda, rather, *Bryn,* had given it to her. If Djuna wanted the entire City of Los Angeles traipsing through to gawk at Brenda, there was not a damn thing Vera could do about it.

Once the visitors began coming, Vera knew, the rhythm of her days would change; no longer the timeless ritual of waiting, while the sun traversed its arc and the sky progressed from white to blue to umber. The quiet, which had been so deep that she got lost in it, so vast that she surrendered to it like a thick and dreamless sleep, would bristle with the din of interruption, the clamor of people and their sympathies. Vera grieved the impending loss of quiet as one might mourn an empty room that had seemed so much more comforting before the furniture arrived. For several days everything had been secure: her chair in its place beside the bed, the unbroken waves of light across her daughter's monitors, the familiar schedule of procedures, each day exactly like the day before. She had almost imagined she could spend the rest of her life in just this way.

Yesterday a new nurse had said to her, "You poor thing, it must be so hard," but the truth was, it was easy, nothing more required than to steep herself in silence and in stillness, allow the time to pass without a sense of expectation. The arrival of visitors would destroy the balance.

The first to call arrived with no forewarning: an unnaturally thin young man with ashy skin, like chocolate left too long in the refrigerator. His somewhat-stockier companion wore the oversized baggy pants and tails-out flannel shirt that Vera had seen worn by gang members on TV. Alarmed, she rose to intercept them; they introduced themselves as Eric and Jorge. She suggested in an icy tone that perhaps they were looking for another room.

Eric moved his slender frame as though his bones were fragile and might break at any moment, but his face remained determined. "They told me room 617. East. I'm here to see Bryn."

Without another word he slid past Vera, dropped into the chair beside the bed. "Yo, Bryn," he murmured in a lustrous tenor, and took her cold hand in his.

"She's our teacher," Jorge explained before Vera could protest further. "She came to see Eric all the time when he was in the hospital last year."

"I'm her mother," Vera countered, although the words held rather less authority than she had hoped. She wasn't sure which aspect of the two men scared her most: their dark complexions and their menacing attire—the hoops and studs that gleamed in their respective ears, the tattoos sprouting in the open collar of a shirt—or the shadow of illness, so prominent in Eric but also now observed in Jorge, that grayed their skin.

Eric had stood again and was examining the plastic bag that hung suspended from the IV stand. "Hey, that's the shit they had me on, remember?"

Jorge nodded in corroboration. "It made him real sick," he concurred, for Vera's benefit.

"There's another kind they can use, but they don't tell you. You gotta ask for it. I'm tellin' you, you gotta be an advocate, you got to question everything they do in here, if you wanna get out alive." Eric fixed his gaze on Vera as if expecting her to take immediate steps.

"What were you . . . uh . . . sick with?" she asked, not knowing what she was supposed to say.

The men exchanged a look she couldn't read before Eric responded, "AIDS. Didn't you know your daughter has a writing class for people with HIV?"

There were many things Bryn had told her that she didn't like to think about. "Well," her voice was edged with a defensive whine, "she teaches other classes too."

"She's a good teacher," Jorge deftly changed the conversation's focus. "She helped a bunch of us to get our work published."

Vera had never seen someone with AIDS, except perhaps on television. She stared at the young men before her, trying to reconcile their physicality with her mental image of a person with the disease. Somehow, she would expect them to look even worse, maybe like the lepers she had heard about in childhood, flesh peeling, their noses dropping off.

"She's the *best* teacher," Eric corrected his friend, "'cuz she loves us." He bent over Bryn's body, inert against the starched white sheet "Remember what you told me?" he said to her, "You said it wasn't time yet; I had more work to do." He shook her gently by the shoulders. "Come on, girlfriend, you gotta fight this! You got a lotta work to do."

He straightened then, and turned his face away, his eyes hard as metal. "This world is fucked up," he declared, and strode abruptly from the room. Vera could hear the rhythmic clatter of his step along the hall.

An awkward silence stretched before Jorge offered, "It's hard on him." He too began inching toward the door. "She was s'posed to be his literary executor; he put it in his will and everything."

The young man broke off then, his eyes darting down the hallway. "Listen, tell Djuna we'll come back, okay? Tell her we want her to come for dinner. You could come too if you want."

He's so polite, Vera found herself thinking as she looked into his sallow face. *He has a mother and she raised him to be polite.* "Thank you," she said, and almost reached to stroke his cheek. "Thank you for coming, and thank Eric too."

"Nice to meet you," he mumbled, and then disappeared.

No more than an hour had passed before the next visitor appeared, a woman Vera's age or older, clad in a jogging suit of magenta silk. Her blond hair was extravagantly coifed, her features sharp, exaggerated by the accumulated stretch of several face-lifts.

"Hi there, you must be Vera." The woman extended a hand that sported several large rings, hunks of gold stippled with real-looking gems, the nails French manicured. "I'm Rose Rifkin; I'm June's mother."

Vera accepted the proffered hand, embarrassed to display her own modest wedding ring, a plain gold band, the only jewelry she wore. A long time ago Chet had splurged on a glittering diamond ring, but six months later he'd wagered and lost it in a poker game. Her fingers scarcely brushed against Rose's, but when she pulled them back they smelled of Rose's perfume, floral and full bodied, expensive, overbearing.

"I'm so sorry I haven't gotten over here till now," Rose continued in her breathless lilt, "but then June tells me they weren't allowing visitors before."

Her sling-back pumps were dyed the same bright color as her outfit; on these she tripped past Vera and approached the bed. "This poor kid!" she announced with lugubrious vigor. "It's a darn shame."

She perched on the edge of the bed and reached for one of Bryn's limp hands, kneading it like a string of worry beads. "I've always just adored Bryn. So sweet, so understanding. June's not like that. Sometimes I think I love your daughter better than I do my own."

She swiveled halfway around to give Vera a conspiratorial wink. "Bryn always *hated* when I said that, but it's true." She expelled a long and wistful sigh. "She's been so good for June."

Vera fingered a button on her old white cardigan, a gift from Bryn at least a decade earlier. It had once been stylish, an impressive garment. Ever since she'd married Everett, it seemed, her daughter had made a point of giving her expensive gifts, as if to highlight Everett's frugality. The sweater was now gray with age, though, and nearly shapeless. Vera felt herself to be no match for this pink-clad woman; she longed to grab her daughter's hand, snatch it back from the grip of square-tipped nails.

"I thought your daughter's name was Djun*a*," was what she said. A flush spread across her cheeks; her comment sounded stupid, maybe even rude beside Rose Rifkin's effusive pronouncements.

There was a sour quality to Rose's smile. "*Some* children," she intoned, "are grateful for the name their parents gave them. Some think they're *lucky* to be born at all. My youngest daughter, June, is not among them."

"Neither is mine," Vera admitted, and at Rose's puzzled look explained, "Her given name is Brenda."

Rose made a tiny sound, not quite a gasp, as she sucked her breath in through her straight white teeth. "I never knew that," she marveled, and although Vera resented the implication that Rose somehow *should* have known this detail of her daughter's life, she joined her in a commiserating laugh.

"And I bet you call her Brenda still," Rose ventured.

"What else?" Vera shrugged. "It's her name."

It was odd to find that she had something in common with this woman, both of them spurned by their offspring in this same way. She had the urge to ask, *Was it hard for you too when your daughter told you she was gay? Do you sometimes search her face, looking for the person you thought you knew?*

But Rose had no time for this exchange of intimacies. Already she was gathering the straps of her magenta handbag; absently she patted Bryn's hand, replaced it by her side, and stood.

"I'm sorry I can't stay." She pouted her cerise lips. "But I'll be back. And Sid and I will definitely have you for supper, very soon. I'll call June and set that up, okay? And you call if you need anything, you promise?"

She pressed her cheek to Vera's and was gone in a blur of pink. Her footsteps were receding down the corridor as Vera raised her hand to wipe her face, moist and sticky now from Rose's touch.

17.

Djuna

Thursday, February 11

"Your mother came today."

This was the news that greeted Djuna as she stepped into the hospital room that evening; it was news she was not thrilled to hear. Already her day seemed to have exceeded its quota of aggravation: a client unsatisfied with the proofs she'd sent him, an outdoor shoot she'd had to cancel when the thick cloud cover of the morning had refused to lift by noon, a parking ticket on her windshield after the aborted shoot, impossible traffic all the way to the hospital. Coming up in the elevator, she'd already begun to feel surly, anticipating Vera's hovering presence, her stricken eyes.

Upon hearing the announcement, Djuna cast her eyes into every corner of the room, lids narrowed, wary, as if some noxious spirit might be left behind, waiting in ambush. She could imagine Rose, dressed in something garish and expensive, taking an hour out from her daylong sojourn at the beauty shop, dashing in and then, just as quickly, dashing out again. Indeed, her nostrils were assailed by the residue of Rose's perfume hanging in the chilled air.

"Did she?" was all that Djuna said, careful to keep her voice neutral. The last thing she wanted was another fight with Vera about allowing visitors to come.

"And a couple of young men—they *said* Bryn knows them—Eric and . . . 'Hor-Jay,' I think; am I saying that right?"

Djuna made herself suppress the grin that formed at the corners of her mouth. She recalled Bryn once saying that her mother was the kind of midwesterner who found pronouncing any word outside the English language an embarrassing affront, the kind who could become unhinged when faced with ordering in an ethnic restaurant.

"Hor-hey," Djuna corrected gently, aware that it would probably do no good. "Bryn will be so happy that they came."

Vera seemed to wince at the use of future tense; it was a way, Djuna noticed, that Vera did not allow herself to speak.

"I worry about those boys," Djuna continued, "Bryn's class has really been important to them. How did they look?"

Vera's expression remained blank, as though the question had thrown her. Eventually she replied, "I guess I don't know how to answer that. They both looked better and worse than I would have imagined."

Djuna nodded, not wanting to pursue it. "I bet they're taking this hard. Damn, I wish I'd seen them."

"They said they'd come back. They said they wanted to have you over."

Djuna made no response and the two stood in an awkward silence.

"Your mom seemed nice," Vera tried again; she sounded tentative, as if she were expecting to be contradicted.

"Did she?" Djuna asked once more, as though she either disagreed with Vera's assessment or else doubted her sincerity.

Bryn had always wanted Vera to meet Rose, "our mothers-in-law," she'd called them with a wicked smile. Djuna had discouraged it out of some instinctive dread, and because Vera had only been to California once in the course of their relationship, it had not been a serious source of conflict.

"She said she'd have us both to dinner," Vera persisted; her voice had leapt a register, taking on a pleading quality.

"I wouldn't bet on it," Djuna sneered. "That's just something she *says,* when she thinks that kind of thing is called for."

Hurt sagged on Vera's face; her features drooped like putty, although whether it was because of Djuna's words or that she had been duped by Rose's charm, Djuna could not be sure. Then something burst forth from behind the sagging cheeks, the way a cloudy sky can suddenly erupt in lightning, a flash of fire in the older woman's eyes.

"I have just about had it with you," Vera announced in a furious hiss. Her face was shifting rapidly, clouds brewing for the squall. Djuna had no chance to run for cover.

"Do you think you're the only one who finds this hard?" Vera's hands were balled into fists; they punched the air. "That's my only daughter in that bed. You two have worked it out so that I have no rights; I can't just pack her up and take her home with me, so if I want to be with her at all, I *have* to stay here.

"I'm tired of you acting like I'm in the way, just another burden you have to put up with, like everything would be just fine if only I would disappear."

Djuna gaped at her, a little frightened but still fascinated. Bryn had talked about her mother's temper, lurking just beneath the surface of that helplessness, but Djuna had never before witnessed it in action.

"Is that what you're trying to do?" Vera demanded, rage strangling her voice into a rasp that rattled in her throat, "Make me get on a plane and go back home and let my daughter die here all alone? Is it? Is it?" She was moving closer, fists circling wider, and for a moment Djuna thought she might be hit, but then Bryn's mother stopped, perhaps two feet away.

Her stance compelled a response, reassurance, an apology, but before Djuna could find her voice they heard a muted knock. The door was open, but Lowell stayed outside, red faced, not sure of whether she should enter.

"Uh . . . is this a bad time?" she stammered. "I can come back."

"Maybe you should give us a few minutes—" Djuna began, but Vera cut her off.

"Lowell!" she exclaimed, and the storm broke. The anger cleared from her brow; her face was now the picture of a sunny day, the sidewalks dry, birds singing, no evidence of the downpour that had passed. "Come right in," she insisted.

"Hi, Djuna," Lowell wrapped her in an uneasy hug, returned by Djuna with the same reserve. They were strangely formal with each other, as if their roles vis-à-vis Bryn required a certain protocol, a good-natured distance. Despite Bryn's fervent reassurance, Djuna harbored a suspicion that her lover would have preferred to be with Lowell still, that she, Djuna, remained a distant runner-up, awarded first place by default. In Lowell's company, Djuna always felt that she was jockeying for position, or scrambling to keep her place.

"And Vera."

Lowell had moved on, was taking Vera's two hands in her own. Pointedly finished with Djuna, Vera was purring, "Lowell, I'm so glad you've come."

18.

Bryn

The wounds are dry now,
their raw scent faded.
A smell like toast,
faint yeast
and charred.
Skin has no memory;
it reinvents itself,
cell by cell.
Even scars
relinquish their stories
in time.
What remains is
the stretched membrane,
pulled thin
so the light shines through.
Can you see the light,
so bright it's blinding?

Skin has no secrets
it can keep,
only what tries
to hide beneath:
the cowardly viscera.
But it can't hide forever.
Cut the skin,
make a wound,
and it's all there
waiting to erupt.

19.

Vera

The restaurant was dark—lit by no more than the glow of candles, flickering on each table in their netted glass—and not too fancy. The air was fragrant with yeast and garlic, and the din of conversation that rose from the cluster of tables seemed both casual and lively. A neighborhood place. A joint. In such an ambiance, Vera could relax, not fret about the dinginess of her old sweater, her ruined hairdo.

She believed that Lowell must have sensed this when she'd suggested dinner. "I know this little place in Laurel Canyon; it's funky, but they have great food. I think you'll like it," she'd assured Vera as she pulled her Jaguar out of the parking garage, flipping on her headlights as if to greet the night.

It was just this kind of sensitivity, a graciousness, that Vera most appreciated about Lowell. It was odd, perhaps, to feel so comfortable with one's daughter's former lover, unusual certainly for Vera, who had never much liked women, who did not make friends easily. But Vera had liked Lowell from their first meeting, that first trip she'd made to California when Brenda had introduced them, declaring proudly, "This is Lowell."

She had visited again while the two were still together, and Lowell had stayed at Vera's house once or twice as well. Even after Brenda no longer lived with Lowell, Vera had continued to send birthday and Christmas cards, to write occasional letters. On her last trip to California, though she'd stayed with Brenda and Djuna, Vera had made a date with Lowell for lunch and a matinee. She'd liked the idea of having a friend of her own in L.A.; it made her feel less dependent on her daughter, upon whose favorable disposition one could never count.

The woman who sat before her now, chewing at her lower lip as she craned the menu toward the sputtery illumination of the candle, was nearly forty-five, but she retained a quality of boyishness that made her seem much younger. Her hair was entirely silver, as it had been—Brenda had once told Vera—since the age of twenty, but it was cut so short and bristly that the color appeared more an affected style than a sign of aging. Her clothes were casual: a T-shirt the color of mustard, loose pants, a jacket, expensive but rumpled. Lowell Bentley was nothing like the few rich people Vera had known in her life, bosses, mostly, and bosses' wives, in their shiny dresses and showy diamonds, their late-model Cadillacs and a twist to their mouths that conveyed their conviction of superiority.

A waiter appeared then with a warm greeting for Lowell, who, after briefly consulting Vera, ordered a bottle of wine. White wine, Vera's request. She marveled at Lowell's facility with the wine list; none of the men she had ever been married to could have told the difference between a Chablis and a Chardonnay. But then, they had not been wine drinkers, and neither had she.

Vera had only begun to drink wine a few years back, after her daughter had accused her of having a drinking problem (Vera would not use Brenda's word for it: alcoholism). It was ridiculous, of course, another idea Brenda had got into her head, another thing to blame her parents for, but Vera had decided at the time it couldn't hurt to cut back on the hard stuff. The entire time she'd been here she hadn't had one drink, except for the vodka she'd sipped on the airplane—she was a nervous flier. Surely her daughter could not object to a glass of wine with dinner.

Lowell was extolling the virtues of the menu, and readily agreed when Vera pleaded, "Why don't you just order for both of us?" They held a brief negotiation over pizza toppings; Vera was certain she did not want artichoke hearts or peppers, Lowell was okay with pepperoni but not with olives.

"Didn't you used to be a vegetarian?" Vera asked her.

Lowell's grin was sheepish as she explained, "When Bryn and I were together, I kind of did it for survival. In those days, whenever someone would eat meat in front of her she'd start talking about dead animals. It wasn't very appetizing."

Vera nodded; she too remembered this phase of her daughter's past.

"After we broke up," Lowell continued, "I was involved for a while with a woman who was a gourmet chef at one of the top restaurants here. I quickly returned to my former carnivorous state."

Vera met her smile, but something stiffened in her spine. The ending of the story seemed somehow to hold a reprimand of Bryn, unspoken yet still palpable, and she wondered if it were disloyal to listen without challenge.

So, too, was she struck by the ease with which Lowell had said the words, "After we broke up," releasing them like fireflies from a Mason jar, setting them free in the night. It signaled an acceptance, an absence of regret, that Vera herself had never learned to feel, not even with her first husband, Carl, Bryn's father, from whom she'd been divorced for almost forty years.

"Are you okay?" Lowell's question broke the reverie into which Vera had begun to drift.

In response she nodded vigorously, said, "I'm fine," and gulped a mouthful of the Fumé Blanc. Her eyelids fluttered closed as the wine eased through her limbs like a balm. She tried to figure out the reason she felt so let down, and then she understood: some part of her had always been harboring the hope that Lowell and her daughter would someday reconcile. The way she and Chet had broken up and gotten back together, twice, three times, before they'd finally called it quits. *Meant to be,* Chet used to say during the good times. That's how she'd thought of Bryn and Lowell. *Meant to be.*

But the quality of resolution in Lowell's voice, the way she could say, "After we broke up," without wincing, without a hint of quaver in her throat, told Vera she'd been wrong, that her dreams of reconciliation would not come to pass.

The ache of disappointment that stirred beneath her rib cage was so pronounced that she longed to repudiate it. "Tell me," she began impulsively, then wished that she could take it back. She hung for just a moment on the strand of indecision, the phrase "Oh, never mind" collecting on her tongue, but Lowell's slate gray eyes were so encouraging that she continued. "Maybe it's none of my business; I was just wondering: Do you ever feel sorry that things didn't work out with the two of you?"

The gray eyes hardened then, not with unkindness but something else, unreadable, with density and mass. Lowell's square hand gripped the stem of the wine glass, tipped it to her lips. "Sorry?" Lowell shrugged. "I wouldn't say that. It's been ten years."

Vera started with that recognition, the passage of time. Ten years since the two had "broken up"? They'd been apart now longer than they'd been a couple. She supposed that was true for her and Chet now, too; eighteen years since the divorce, after fifteen years of marriage. Soon she would have been married to Everett for as long as she'd been to Chet. That was not possible.

Something in her torso felt as if it were giving way, the architecture of her ribs collapsing, crumbling to dust. Vera groped for her wine glass, drained it, as if the liquid it contained were glue and could hold together her dissolving parts. The waiter appeared instantly to pour a refill.

Lowell, too, was emptying her glass, starting on another. She seemed not to be aware of Vera's distress; almost to herself she mused, "Bryn was never easy. I don't think I'm telling you anything you don't know when I say she is very intense."

Vera bobbed her head; she couldn't disagree. Lowell took another sip before continuing. "Our last few years together were really hard. You know, she had all those affairs."

This, too, jolted Vera, shooting like a current through her body, leaving her mouth dry as ash. Had she known this and forgotten? She couldn't think just now what Brenda had said about their ending, but Vera could remember clearly how distraught her daughter had been, the tear-choked voice on the telephone. Or was it she who had cried? Vera tried to reconcile her memory with Lowell's revelation; surely this woman had no reason to lie to her.

"I'm sorry," Lowell's mouth stretched to an embarrassed grin. "I didn't mean to drop a bomb on you."

"Well," Vera managed a self-deprecating laugh, "My daughter has told me that I only remember things the way I want them to have happened. Tell me again," she urged.

A look of doubt crossed over Lowell's face like a small cloud. "It's not a pretty story," she warned. "I don't know what Bryn would think about my telling you all this. Are you sure. . . . ?"

Vera understood that she was at a threshold; she could stop now, remain on the other side, or she could cross over. Like Eve, she reflected; was this knowledge that she wasn't meant to have? It was not simple curiosity that moved her forward, nor was it courage—Vera would have been the first to admit that she was not brave. What propelled her now was much more base; it shamed her to admit it to herself. For years she had listened while her daughter castigated her mistakes, enumerating the myriad bad choices, the flagrant errors in judgment of which Vera had been guilty, tallying the consequences that had befallen Brenda as a result of her mother's failings. On Vera's last visit, Brenda had dragged her before her therapist, as though she needed another witness to the recitation of crimes. In all that time she had never heard her daughter talk about her own mistakes, her flaws, their repercussions. What Lowell offered now seemed like a gift, as rare as it was forbidden, and Vera snatched it greedily, saying, "Please, go on."

Lowell sighed into the bell of the wine glass. With a grimace she confessed, "This is one of those conversations that makes me wish I still smoked cigarettes."

Then she looked away from Vera, aimed her eyes at nothing but the darkness of the room. "There were at least four that I know about," she admitted, "not including a flirtation with her therapist that I'm pretty sure was never consummated."

"Not the therapist she made me go to see with her?" Vera's mouth hung in an O of indignation.

"No, no," Lowell hastened to calm her. "A different therapist, a long time ago. A real slimeball, if you ask me." She paused to gulp the dregs of her glass. "Are you *sure* you want to hear this?"

Misgivings hissed in a corner of Vera's brain, but she could not stop now. Once, when Brenda was about thirteen, Vera had sneaked into her room and read her diary. She no longer knew what she might have been expecting to find: confessions of an adolescent crush, perhaps, or admissions of petty crimes. She had been chagrined to read instead a detailed account of a fight between herself and Chet; it had seemed so brutal and so vicious, rendered in her daughter's hand. Vera had never snooped again. But Lowell's story promised to implicate no one but Brenda; here at last was something for which Vera could not be blamed. It was irresistible. "Go on," she insisted, urgency tightening her throat.

"So anyway," Lowell picked up the thread of her story as she refilled both their glasses, "the first affair was right in the beginning. I hated it, but I felt *I* was to blame; I was still going back and forth with my ex, and it was making Bryn crazy. So she decided to give me a taste of my own medicine, and at the time I guess I figured I had it coming."

Salads were set before them, pungent with fresh herbs, strong vinegar. At the first bite a burst of saliva swarmed on Vera's tongue; she had been eating little these past weeks, and only what was provided by the hospital cafeteria, nothing to incite her taste buds. Lowell had pulled off a chunk of the crusty bread that nestled between them in a plastic basket; once she had chewed and swallowed she resumed her recitation.

"The next one went on a long time, probably three years. Bryn lied to me about it the whole time, and I let myself believe her. I'd tell myself I was just paranoid, I should learn to be more trusting, that my suspicions didn't mean anything, you know?"

Vera nodded; she did know. She'd done the same, for years, with Chet. Believing all the stories: "I had to work late," "I got drunk and slept in the car," "I was playing poker with the boys" till dawn. Holding hostage the part of her that knew the truth, keeping it bound and gagged, locked in a dark closet like Patty Hearst, until, like the kidnapped heiress, it was easier to just believe her captors. Her need to believe Chet growing stronger, fierce, with every lie.

"Then there was one with a woman from Michigan, someone Bryn had known before she moved to California."

Yes, Vera thought; she had even met that one, when Brenda was on a visit home. The three of them had gone to lunch. Vera wondered if she'd realized then that her daughter and the thin, dark-haired woman were involved, and what she'd done with that awareness at the time. She wondered too if Lowell would think her traitorous if she knew about that lunch.

"And then there was the last one." A napkin twisted in Lowell's square hand, the fabric taut, the knuckles white. "My last straw. Bryn had decided it was 'damaging'—to her, of course—for her to lie, so this time she looked me in the face and told me where she was going, what she was going to do, and when she'd be home in the morning. I told her not to bother." Again, the shrug. "I guess I'd finally had enough."

Enough. The word lodged in Vera's ear like an old, familiar melody. Enough. When the heart grows so bitter that it seems to empty. Enough.

Their dinner was delivered to the table then, the pizza redolent of spicy pepperoni and tomato sauce, steam rising from its rounded face, the cheese still bubbling like a molten lake. It wasn't only appetite that made the women hail its arrival; both welcomed the distraction, the relief from further conversation. They set upon the pizza as if ravenous, dragging thick triangles from its aluminum tray, stuffing the points between their teeth and chewing furiously.

Although she offered praise for its rich flavors, Vera scarcely tasted what she swallowed. She tried to concentrate on Brenda, this new and troubling portrait Lowell had painted of her only child, but her thoughts kept returning to Chet. He had screwed around, had lied to her, and maybe even worse, but she had never learned to hate him. It was not hatred that had finally driven them apart, but exhaustion, a weariness love could not overcome. Lowell seemed to evidence that same fatigue talking about Bryn, but clearly she did not despise her.

Lowell poured the last of the bottle into her glass and signaled the waiter for another. Without meeting Vera's gaze, she began to tell about a recent trip she'd taken, three weeks in Bali, her cheerful travelogue erasing all that had come before.

Between mouthfuls, Vera eyed her companion, surreptitious as a co-conspirator. She could not help but wonder what her daughter would have made of this discussion; would she have accused them of betrayal, of gossiping behind her back? Or would she have been gratified, oddly pleased to be the focus of their conversation, to find herself the center of attention?

20.

Djuna

After the rapturous departure of Bryn's mother with Bryn's ex-lover, Djuna was left alone. Alone with the maddening buzz of monitors, the din of traffic in the corridor, alone with her lover's unreachable spirit. A nurse had come to turn Bryn's body, now resting on its right side, face aimed toward the curtained window. A pulse beat in Djuna's temple, a merciless drum.

Her fist thumped the bed and the IV tubes danced. The river of rage she had traveled the day before in Evelyn's office opened in her body once again. "Goddamn it," she snarled at the recumbent form, "it's all your fault." Someone was surely to blame for the upending of her life. "Everything's completely fucked, and it's all your fault."

Evelyn had said it was important to express her feelings, but Djuna's outburst brought her neither comfort nor relief. Her words seemed to glance off her lover's skin, as if the pale flesh had thickened to armor. Those words bounced back against Djuna's ear; they sounded callous, brutish, like the dumb roar of a vengeful bull set loose in this room of fragile things. The way Vera saw her. Not refined like Lowell.

Lowell, who, despite Vera's efforts to monopolize her, had bent over the bed, smoothed an errant lock of hair back from Bryn's forehead, whispered, "Hey you, what's all this?" with a mix of tenderness and restraint. Who had Lowell seen, as she picked up a tissue to wipe the crust from the corner of Bryn's eyes—the woman who'd once been her lover, the woman Bryn had subsequently become, or a rag doll who was no one, who might never be someone again?

Djuna would never know the answer to this; Vera had allowed Lowell only a few minutes before she'd begun to pester her for attention. Lowell, ill at ease with the tension crackling in the air, had allowed Vera to steer her from the room.

Now futility leaned its full weight against Djuna, until it seemed she would be crushed. The impulse to flee erupted in her limbs, but before she could make her escape, Emily's face peered in through the door.

"I hope I'm not interrupting," she burbled with a toss of her shoulder-length hair. "I'm sorry I'm so late; I had therapy," she explained. Emily went to therapy more than anyone Djuna had ever known—three times a week. A lapsed Catholic, Emily had a faith in therapy that bordered on the religious. Djuna could never imagine how Emily managed to afford it.

Breathless and contrite, Emily entered, her petite figure still clothed in the uniform of workaday life, a trim navy business suit and pumps of a sensible height. With her honey brown hair in a smooth pageboy, her Slavic features kissed with just a hint of makeup, Emily was one of those women whose lesbianism was not, on the surface, obvious. She looked the part of an attractive, no-nonsense businesswoman, which masked her highly unusual mind.

In addition to her stylish handbag, Emily carried a knapsack slung over one shoulder and toted a huge boom box in her other hand. Leaving them strewn on the floor, she greeted Djuna with a brief, distracted hug, less an embrace than a quick banging together of bodies.

She pulled away and made a beeline for the bed, enveloping Bryn in the fierce clutch of her arms. "Girl, I am *so glad* to see you!" She spoke at full conversational volume, as if she had every reason to expect an answer. "I'm telling you, when you get out of here, you're gonna march right back to that lawyer and add *my* name to that power of attorney for health care. They kept me out, honey, that's the only reason I wasn't here nine days ago."

Djuna could not help but contrast Emily's heartiness with her own tentative murmurings to Bryn. She could scarcely fathom that effusion of energy, which seemed to have its own momentum, an engine that did not require the fuel of Bryn's response.

"Who cut this hair?" Emily demanded, running her fingers through the shorn locks that now contained as much silver as gold.

She'd directed the question to Bryn, but it was Djuna who replied, "They did it in the emergency room when they first examined her, and then Vera evened it out."

Emily snorted. "Well, it looks like the kind of haircut somebody's mother would give them." To Djuna she complained, "Bryn will have a fit to have her hair looking like this. You should at least get Rico in here to give it some shape." Rico was the stylist both Emily and Bryn had been going to for the last ten years. Djuna gave her an incredulous look, but Emily wore the expression of someone who'd just made a completely sensible suggestion and expected to see it enacted without delay.

"I . . . uh . . . I don't think it's gonna make much of a difference right now," Djuna raised her palms in an appeal to reason.

In a decisive few steps, Emily moved to Djuna and took her by the shoulders. Despite her smaller stature, her body conveyed authority. "Djuna, you listen to me. Your girlfriend is alive, you got that? She's the same person she's always been. A *person*, you hear me, not a *thing*. If you treat her like a thing, with no feelings, no preferences, then that's what she'll turn into. I've been reading about this," she released her grip on Djuna and bent to retrieve her knapsack. Unzipping the main pouch, she extracted a thick sheaf of pages, computer printouts.

"There are all these stories of miraculous recovery from coma," she fanned the pages in Djuna's direction, "and the one thing they all have in common is this: somebody loved the person in the coma enough to make extraordinary efforts, to fight the doctors, to never give up."

She delivered the stack of papers into Djuna's hands with the firm conviction of an attorney presenting the judge with indisputable evidence. "I normally try to mind my own business about things, but this is too important to worry about being appropriate."

Then she returned to Bryn's side, squealing, "I brought you a few things." From the depths of the knapsack, she pulled a bottle of cologne, Bryn's favorite, and sprayed it lavishly against Bryn's neck and across her pillow. As the scent diffused in the room, Djuna's eyes filled with tears; she hadn't even realized how much she'd missed that smell.

Emily next produced a quilted, antique bed jacket of shell-pink satin. Holding it up for Djuna's inspection, Emily recalled, "We practically got into a catfight over this one time at the Long Beach swap meet. That was before she knew you. In the end, she won, but after she bought it, she gave it to me. Here, help me with this."

Djuna lifted Bryn by the shoulders while Emily gingerly guided one of Bryn's arms through the sleeve of the bed jacket. When she tried the left arm, though, she was defeated by the tubes that connected Bryn's body to the bank of machines. Instead, Emily had to be content with draping the garment over Bryn's left shoulder. They eased her down onto the pillows, then Emily stood back to admire the effect. "Oh, honey," she cooed, "It always did look better on you anyway." Djuna was struck by the way the pink brought out a blush of color in Bryn's face, which had seemed so waxy just a moment before.

Emily next added a dab of lipstick to Bryn's mouth, the deep raisin color Bryn loved to wear. "Next time I come," Emily promised her, "We'll do a full beauty makeover. I tell you, girlfriend, that's why you gotta put *me* on your documents. You can't trust a butch to tend to the important details like this!"

Finally, Emily returned to the door and lugged the compact disc player to the bedside table. From the knapsack she pulled a CD, Miles Davis's *Kind of Blue*. The next minute the room was full of the torchy melancholy of "So What."

"I brought a bunch of different things," she explained, placing a stack of CDs next to the player. Idly, Djuna thumbed the selection: the music of Erik Satie, Tito Puente's Latin jazz, Marvin Gaye, Aretha. There was even a recording of music played on Himalayan bowls.

"You got all her favorites," Djuna said; she was both touched and shamed by the extent of Emily's efforts.

"Well, I did overlook her heavy-metal fetish." Emily grinned, "I thought the hospital might not be amused."

"Not to mention Vera," Djuna added, and for the first time that day her face relaxed into a genuine smile.

Her mission accomplished, Emily now turned her full attention to Djuna, probing her with blue eyes that were slightly magnified by her tortoise-shell glasses. "So tell me how *you* are," she commanded, wrapping Djuna in a real hug until Djuna broke away, trying to blink back the tears that pooled in the corners of her eyes.

"You can tell me all about it," Emily soothed, "Have you had dinner?"

Djuna shrugged. "Dinner" might as well have been some custom from an alien planet with which she had no familiarity.

"Come on," Emily suggested, "Let's go someplace where we can eat and talk."

She returned once more to the bed, bending down to rest her cheek against Bryn's head. She might have been whispering a secret into

Bryn's ear; Djuna could not tell for sure. Emily straightened, stood, and drew apart the window curtains to reveal the vista of the city night. Beyond the pane of glass glowed the lights of the Hollywood Hills.

"A girl needs to enjoy the view," she explained, as if she were expecting Djuna to argue. She turned the volume just a little higher, said, "Good-bye, honey, I'll be back," and reached for Djuna's hand.

Djuna followed, grateful to be led, but as they neared the door, they heard a low moan, muffled and otherworldly, at their backs. Both women whirled around in the same instant, as if this were a movement they had practiced, a step in some elaborate routine that brought them to the foot of Bryn's bed. Although neither of them could have said what she expected to find, each registered dejection upon seeing that the body in the bed remained unchanged. Djuna's shoulders sagged, and she saw the crestfallen look that dimmed Emily's features. Bryn's posture was no different than it had been just a moment earlier, her face still pale and blank but for the dark lips that seemed to glow in a field of white.

Both Emily and Djuna fixed their gaze on that bright swatch of color, waiting, without breath. Finally, Djuna nudged Emily's ribs. "Did you hear that too?" she asked, her voice almost a whisper.

"I think I did." It was the first time that day that Djuna found uncertainty in Emily's manner.

"You're sure it wasn't just something in the music?"

"Not unless they've added something to this CD that was never there before."

Neither took her eyes from Bryn's mouth. The ambling piano of "Freddie Freeloader" had begun, countered by Miles's blistering horn. When sound came once more from Bryn it was more of a whimper, and the mouth did not move at all; only the eyelids, still closed, seemed to press together more tightly, as if wincing.

"Get the nurse," Djuna barked at Emily, who obeyed without challenge. With a jab of her fist, Djuna punched the CD player off; the music evaporated in the air as she strained her ears to catch whatever new sounds Bryn might make.

"Pie, I'm right here." She perched on the edge of the bed and cradled the side of Bryn's face in one hand. "Does anything hurt you? Come on, baby, stay with me. Tell me what you need."

Breathless, Emily returned, pulling a nurse in tow. Djuna was grateful to see it was the good nurse, Mark, a freckled strawberry blond with a small gold hoop through his left ear. Djuna liked him because he got it about her relationship to Bryn—he never deferred to Vera the way the older day nurse did—and because he usually had a smile and a joke at hand.

Now, though, his expression was serious as Emily insisted, "She's making noises, she's trying to wake up! *Do* something! Help her!"

The figure on the bed belied this claim; Bryn's features had returned to blankness, and the only sounds emitting from her were the soft breaths that whistled through her nostrils.

"What happened to the music?" Emily demanded. "We put on some music and Bryn started to wake up." She punched the power button on the CD player; "So What" began anew.

"Come on, Bryn, *listen*," Emily hissed. Djuna had to marvel at Emily's sense of her own power, the way she seemed convinced she could affect the course of events. Still, despite her urgings, Bryn remained immutable.

Mark looked to Djuna for some explanation. Her chest felt cramped, as if her lungs were slowly deflating, collapsing like hope. She could scarcely find the breath to speak.

"First she moaned. Then a few minutes later she kind of whimpered." Djuna tried to mimic the noise she had heard. "Her face clenched up for a second, like maybe she was in pain. Then . . . nothing."

Thoughtfully, Mark studied the readings on the monitors. With his delicate fingers he grasped Bryn's wrist and counted softly to himself as he took her pulse. He checked the tubes carrying fluids to and from her body, and took her temperature.

"There doesn't seem to be any physiological change in her condition," he reported at the conclusion of his ministrations. "Her temperature is slightly above normal, but it's been that way consistently since she was brought in; her pulse is steady. All I can really do is write this up on her chart; you can talk to the doctor about it in the morning."

"Don't you think you ought to get a doctor in here now?" Emily's voice was icy; it gouged at Djuna like a sharp chunk of glass.

Mark seemed to choose his next words carefully. "Oftentimes, a patient in a coma will grunt, or groan, or sometimes even speak, the way people will talk in their sleep. These things are all viewed as involuntary sounds—"

"They weren't involuntary," Emily snapped, "We played her music that she knows and likes and she *responded*. I'd hardly call that 'involuntary.'"

Shut up, Djuna wanted to tell her, *he's on our side.* It occurred to her that this must be how Vera felt whenever Djuna started arguing with the doctors.

The nurse's face flushed to the roots of his red-gold hair, but he forced a smile onto his lips as he responded, "Look, I'm sympathetic to what you're saying. I pray every night that your friend here is gonna wake up and be okay. But we can't know for sure if the sounds she made were in response to the music, or to something in her own mind, or to nothing at all. These things tend not to be . . . significant."

"Not significant?" Emily was nearly yelling. Her face grew dangerous. Djuna was afraid her friend was about to shove the nurse, slam into his slender chest with her fists, and she placed a restraining hand on Emily's elbow.

"Thanks, Mark," she said, signaling that he was free to go.

"I'm sorry—" he began, but she waved him away as Emily collapsed in her arms, shoulders heaving, tears soaking into the cloth of her starched shirt.

21.

Djuna

Thursday, February 11

It was Emily who'd picked this place, this cafe that was also a flower shop, where the odor of fresh-brewed coffee mingled with the heady perfume of cut roses. It was Emily who'd suggested it, Djuna who had not been paying sufficient attention to object. She'd followed obediently behind Emily's squat Saab, oblivious to familiar landmarks and traffic signals, turning where Emily turned, braking when Emily braked.

Throughout the short journey, east on Beverly past Fairfax to La Brea, a southward turn to Sixth, Djuna thought only of Bryn and the feeble noises that had shattered the silence of days, like the first music at the beginning of the world. It stunned her that already she could not remember their exact quality, their pitch and timbre; although the sounds played and replayed in Djuna's brain, with each passing heartbeat they grew more vague, shapeless, fading from earshot.

Like Emily, she rejected the notion that Bryn's noises were involuntary, random, meaningless as sighs or farts. Something was trying to be communicated, Djuna was certain.

Sometimes, when faced with a clamoring Toulouse, Bryn would demand of the animal, "Speak English. Tell me what you want in a language *I* can understand." That's what Djuna had said to Bryn, back in the hospital room. But nothing she said, and none of Emily's entreaties, could coax another peep out of Bryn. Perhaps she was angry, Djuna thought, at their failure to comprehend.

It was not until both women had parked their cars, side by side in the lot, and walked into the cafe through the back door, past rows of vases filled with early tulips in a dozen hues, the first daffodils and bundled irises, not until they'd noticed everywhere the dangling paper hearts proclaiming, "Don't forget your valentine on February 14," that Djuna's face constricted like a fist. The lurid cutout cupids pasted to the walls seemed to aim their darts directly at her own fragile ventricles.

Observing the trajectory of Djuna's gaze, Emily grimaced in apology. "I'm sorry; I don't know what I was thinking. Do you want to go someplace else?"

Djuna shook her head and claimed a corner table. It was the table she and Bryn most often chose when they met here each week for dinner after Bryn's class on Wednesday night. It was comforting for Djuna to assume her customary stool beside the dark windows, comforting and terrible.

Emily had gone to place their order and to wash her hands. The server arrived with their meal before she returned. Djuna studied the food without appetite, imagining it as a composition she might photograph. She picked at a lettuce leaf that hung from the edge of her salad plate, stroked it absently between her thumb and forefinger while a bowl of carrot soup cooled in front of her.

"You eat this," Emily ordered, handing her a soup spoon as she climbed aboard the opposite stool. She removed her eyeglasses, folding them tidily beside the edge of her plate. Without them she looked younger and more vulnerable. Some slight blush along the eyelids led Djuna to suspect that Emily had been crying in the bathroom, but all other evidence had been repaired. Spearing a forkful of pasta, Emily commanded, "Now talk to me."

Djuna slid a spoonful of soup between her lips, noting the velvet grain of pureed carrots against her tongue. She swallowed without registering flavor; still, its warmth provoked a relaxation of her muscles, an ease she hadn't felt all day, and for an instant, she drifted.

Fingers snapped in front of her nose. "Come on, girlfriend, give it up. Tell me what you're thinking," Emily insisted.

Djuna shrugged. "I was thinking about the first time I met Bryn. I'm sure you've heard the story. . . ."

Emily suppressed a grin. "Only about fifty times. But tell me again."

"It was during the time when I was taking pictures for *Lesbian Life*. Do you remember that magazine?"

"Who doesn't?" Emily rolled her eyes, "Lavender journalism at its finest. That paper was responsible for more scummy rumors than the *National Enquirer*," she snorted.

Djuna chuckled in agreement. "Anyway, my ex, Charlene—you've never met her, she stopped speaking to me after Bryn and I got together—was on a big campaign to get me to 'do more for the community.' We'd been broken up for a few years but she was still trying to improve me! So she talked me into volunteering to shoot photos for the *Life*. This of course was before I found out that the other photographers got paid, not much, but *something,* and before I found out that Charlene was sleeping with the editor."

"Keep eating," Emily cautioned, as Djuna paused for breath. To mollify her, Djuna tore a hunk from her baguette, but the crusty bread never made it to her lips.

"So, it's awful, right? The women who published that magazine were complete bitches, and the printing was always so bad that my photos looked like shit, and every time I did a shoot for them I swore it would be the last. Then one day they asked me to go and shoot this writer by the name of Bryn Redding. I'd heard her name around the community, but I'd never met her. It was right around the time that her short-story collection was published, and the *Life* decided to raise their standards for once and do a profile of her."

Djuna interrupted her story long enough to drain her water glass; the ice cubes clinked as they hit the empty bottom.

"So, I show up at her house to take this picture, and this woman comes to the door in a black velvet dress, off the shoulder, really low cut, I mean, *sexy.* I couldn't believe it! And of course, she's gorgeous—not exactly the kind of woman I'm used to seeing in the pages of *Lesbian Life*. Maybe I even blushed, I don't know, but she catches my reaction right away, and then she gives me this wicked kind of smile and says, 'I always wear a dress when I'm going to be in some kind of dyke thing. It really messes up their minds.' That's what she said!"

"That was about the time she was going around telling everybody she was a 'militant femme,'" Emily recalled. She reached for Djuna's baguette and broke off a portion for herself.

"Okay, I think, whatever. So I'm setting up my tripod and my lights—this is when she was living in that funky little guest cottage in Echo Park, and I was wondering how in hell I was going to get a decent shot with all the clutter in that place—when she says, 'I really hate to have my picture taken. I never know what to do with my body. But I'm very, very good at following directions, so just tell me whatever you want me to do, and I'll do it.'"

"Oo-wee, baby," Emily used her napkin to fan herself.

"I didn't know how to take it. I mean, was this babe really flirting with me, or what? So I started shooting, and just like she said, she's really tense, and I'm trying to get her to relax, right? So I'm saying, 'Stand here, okay, why don't you sit, put your arms like this, look over here,' you know, the standard things. And out of the blue she says, 'What if I bring my knees up, and rest my chin on them?' So I think, fine, do whatever you want. Next thing I know, she brings her knees to her chin, giving me a full view of what's under her skirt, and Emily, I swear, she's got nothing on."

"You mean no underwear?" Emily's jaw dropped slightly.

"Nothing. Just a panoramic picture of the most intimate part of her anatomy," Djuna insisted.

"She never told me that part of it!" Emily appeared to be more shocked by this withholding than by Bryn's exhibitionism.

"I swear it's true. And it scared the shit out of me. Never in my life had anyone been *that* forward with me. I think I just clammed up at that point. I finished off my roll of film and got out of there as fast as I could. I drove right back to the *Lesbian Life* office and told them it was the last assignment I could do for them."

"What happened to the pictures?" Emily wanted to know.

"At first I was just going to hand them over to the magazine and let Bryn worry about her reputation, but the next day I got a call from her, apologizing. She said she'd wanted to play a joke on the editor, but afterward she realized she'd embarrassed me. She felt bad, she said, and could she take me out to lunch and make it up to me?"

Djuna sighed. Her fingers were crumbling bits of baguette into the congealing pool of soup. "And to think, I almost turned her down."

"Bryn's not an easy woman to say no to," Emily ran a reassuring hand along her friend's arm.

Djuna's vision blurred suddenly, her eyes flooding. "Emily, if I lose her I don't know what I'll do." She dabbed at her face with a napkin and tried to contain the tremors that shook her thin shoulders.

Emily slid her stool closer and wrapped an arm around Djuna. "You won't lose her," she insisted, "She's gonna be okay." She spoke as if she had no doubt.

Emily stared at the plates of uneaten food in front of Djuna. "Right now, you're the one I'm worried about. You've got to eat; you're getting way too thin."

Djuna stared mournfully at her abdomen. "Bryn always said I was too skinny when she met me. After we moved in together, she always made me eat three meals a day."

"What are you down to now?" Emily scolded, "Two? One?"

Djuna ducked her chin. "I'm just not interested in food."

Emily disappeared from the table, returning a few minutes later bearing two cups of French-roast decaf and a brownie studded with walnuts. A spark lit Djuna's eyes as she spied the square of cake; Emily pushed the plate in her direction.

"Here, I was hoping to find something that would tempt you."

Tilting her coffee cup, Djuna swallowed the dark brew, felt it seep into her system like necessary fuel. She was overcome with gratitude for Emily's kind and practical friendship. She broke off a corner of the brownie and popped it into her mouth, let the chocolate ooze between her teeth. Saliva rushed to greet the burst of flavor, teeth ground nuts into grit, her stomach eagerly welcoming this sustenance; all the parts of her present and accounted for, working in the way they were intended. For an instant, life seemed almost normal.

Her tears returned, unaccountably, and she pushed the plate away from her. She turned her concentration to the scene beyond the window, cars streaking up La Brea to unimaginable destinations.

Emily reached for Djuna's hand, the one with the gold band on its third finger. Djuna allowed her hand to be enfolded in Emily's soft grasp, but would not, would not, meet her eyes, so blue, so full of pity.

22.

Bryn

Flames burst
like blossoms,
sunflower bright,
golden spires
that curl and spread,
petals
kindled with light.
Flames cover my body
like fingers,
fan over my flesh.
Lap at my skin
like waves.
Am I swimming?
Is the shore in sight?
Shoreline that winds
like a wick,
rimming
a combustible sea.
I dive.
I drink.
Fire's kiss
possesses me,
rolls its tongue
down my throat
like heavy syrup,
ruptures my eyeballs
like egg yolks,
their yellow stain
like tears.
Fire blesses me,
its brilliance

sanctifies my sins.
Flames illumine me;
everywhere is light,
but no warmth.
Relentless tongues of ice.
I am cold all the time.

23.

Djuna

Sunday, February 14

She'd been waiting for a dream, but when it came she could not, at first, distinguish it from waking. She thought she smelled smoke, and started up from the sweat-drenched pillow. She had seen the gleam of fire seeping through the crack beneath the bedroom door, had flung that door wide to meet a roaring wall of flame, the hallway consumed, timbers twisted and black, the roof caved in, no exit. Heat had singed her eyelashes. Sparks had hissed in her hair.

Djuna squinted in the gray light of the bedroom. Her eyes sought the illuminated face of the clock; its digits glowed like embers. 4:17. Beyond the open door, the hallway loomed silent and dark.

A damp breeze filtered through the window and brought with it the hollow scent of fog. The blankets had slipped to Djuna's waist; gooseflesh pebbled her skin, her small nipples erect. Still shadowed by the dream, her breath was coming too fast. As she leaned against the slatted headboard, she noticed she was trembling.

If Bryn were here beside her, Djuna would awaken her, rolling over to rest her cheek against Bryn's shoulder, whispering, "Honey, I had a bad dream." And Bryn would rouse herself good-naturedly, enough at least to run a soothing hand through Djuna's hair and murmur, "Tell me."

It would always ease Djuna to talk about it; she needed not to be alone with the frightening visions, to set free the nightmares from the confines of her head. It didn't matter that sometimes Bryn would fall back to sleep before Djuna had finished; it was the act of telling that slowly siphoned the fear from her muscles, that confirmed her escape from that threatening landscape, her re-entry into waking life.

Quiet echoed around her, the constant hum of the nearby freeway like white noise underneath the hush. In this moment Djuna could not have said that the crackle of flame was any more sinister than the still half-light of the empty room.

Toulouse dozed in the middle of Bryn's pillow, a spot he'd claimed ever since the accident. Djuna resettled herself in the bed, once more reclined against the flannel sheets. She nestled her cheek experimentally on the cat's soft flank, withholding her full weight. Toulouse lolled on his side and stretched, displacing her, then curled like a halo around her head. The heat of his body surrounded her scalp like a fur hat.

"Toulouse," she began in a plaintive voice, "I had an awful dream."

It wasn't the same, though. With only the tabby as witness, she could not give voice to the fiery pictures that haunted her sleep, as though by speaking she might invoke and not dispel them, might cause the nightmare world to bleed irretrievably into this one.

Unwilling to succumb to sleep, she hauled her body from the mattress and padded, naked, to the kitchen. Her fingers scrabbled for the light switch. The glare of the overhead bulb blackened the night beyond the windows, erased all promise of morning.

Toulouse had followed her into the kitchen, confused by this activity at such an unaccustomed hour, in thrall at the prospect of an unscheduled snack. He stood expectantly before his empty dish, a low purr rumbling in his throat.

Listless, Djuna tugged at the refrigerator door. She shivered as the chilled air blasted her bare flesh. The scene inside was a kind of nightmare itself, dismal as a slum, brimming with refuse and neglect. The squalid remains of wilted lettuce sagged against a bundle of yellowed broccoli. A chunk of cheese sported powdery bruise-colored mold, and the stench of soured milk hung over the shelves like a chemical sky. Cartons of tofu, yogurt, and cottage cheese languished untouched, their long-past expiration dates stamped like indictments on their plastic lids.

Djuna swung shut the door and slumped to the linoleum, her back against the refrigerator's blank metal face. Toulouse approached her with a questioning mew and Djuna scooped him into her lap; for once, he complied without protest, even as Djuna's tears dripped into the fur at his neck.

They sat that way for a long time while the sky lightened and the birds took up their songs. Djuna's muscles grew stiff from the cold floor; her legs fell asleep under the cat's limp weight in her lap.

She had asked for a dream, she reminded herself, had petitioned Bryn's elusive spirit for a sign to staunch her loneliness. Again the flames rose in her vision, consuming this house that she and Bryn had shared, leaving her lungs scorched, her mouth gritty with ash. Was this scene of utter loss and devastation the response to her request?

Carefully she unwound her limbs and struggled to her feet, unsteady as one learning to walk anew. Toulouse made a squeak of complaint, then resumed his post at the supper dish. As she bent to ladle a fistful of crunchies into the red bowl, her eyes fell on the calendar Bryn had tacked above the sink. Accustomed to its presence, year after year, Djuna never looked at it.

Now something drew her, rows of empty boxes except for one, its blankness marred with pencil marks. That square housed today's date: Sunday, February 14. Across its tidy surface was scrawled, in Bryn's jagged, unmistakable hand, "Don't forget how much you're loved, my valentine."

24.

Vera

The small stack of books remained untouched at Vera's bedside for days after Lowell had given them to her. During their dinner together, Lowell had made reference to a poem of Bryn's and Vera, blank faced, had confessed she did not know her daughter's work.

Then she had amended, "Brenda always used to write little poems when she was a kid; they were real cute. I bet I still have some of them tucked away somewhere." Lowell had been gracious, politely masking her surprise and offering to swing by the house and retrieve the books from her library.

There were four books altogether: two volumes of poetry, published a decade apart, a paperbound collection of short stories with the title *Dangerous Truths,* and a slim hardbound novel. The back of its dust jacket showed a small photograph of Bryn; she wore the same tight, self-conscious smile she'd had in every snapshot since childhood, a smile that involved the muscles of the cheeks but not the spirit of the smiler.

When Lowell had first placed them in her hands, Vera made a show of examining the books, making prideful noises as she turned over their covers, remarking at the titles. Once back at the hotel, however, she'd found herself absent of curiosity, relieved to simply observe them as objects, four rectangular blocks that required no interaction.

Their colors glowed beneath the lamp on the bedside table. She regarded them with the same wariness with which she approached wrapped presents: as long as their wrappings remained intact, she could savor their promise, but she never lost the lurking sense of dread about what they might actually contain once stripped of their bright skins.

Vera had maintained her daily vigil at Brenda's side, although that solace was now shattered by a persistent stream of visitors, a tribe of strangers, each claiming some piece of her daughter. Their regard for

Vera was polite but without deference, as though *they* had more right to her daughter than she. They touched Brenda's body with proprietary hands and joked about experiences Brenda had never bothered to disclose to Vera. They obliterated Brenda, invoked instead this changeling Bryn, a woman Vera scarcely knew, but knew enough to fear.

The books remained behind, waiting, patient as abandoned children, for her return each night. Their covers were more vivid than the muted pastels of hotel decor, standing out from every other item in the room, commanding her attention. As the days passed, the books did not disappear; nor did they recede into the landscape, becoming no less conspicuous than the hairbrush atop the bureau, the glass beside the sink. Instead their vigor seemed to grow, to pulse; the books seemed almost to emit a sound, a hum that she could never entirely drown, a muttering that spoke to her in sleep.

Without quite realizing she was doing it, Vera tried a variety of strategies to obscure their presence, covering them with her hand mirror or a box of tissues; once in bed she would stare hard at the television screen, refusing to allow her gaze to stray in their direction, and she kept the volume high. She might have tucked them in her suitcase, out of sight, but she did not; somehow she could not dismiss them so forthrightly.

On this night she could have sworn that they awakened her, as if someone had been shaking her by the shoulder, hissing in her ear. Surfacing abruptly from her troubled sleep, she reached for the light and saw them gleaming up at her, expectant, cheerfully insistent. "It's time," they seemed to say.

The clock read 2:00 A.M.; she'd been sleeping no more than an hour. With a groan she pulled her body from the mattress; the chilled night air seeped through the flannel of her striped pajamas, and a shiver raised the fine hair on her arms.

Fueled with a sudden determination, Vera padded to the room's squat mini-bar, a small refrigerator built into a cabinet of carved wood. Until this moment she'd avoided this appliance, owing less to her vague intentions of sobriety than to her outrage that the items stocked within were sold at twice the price. Now both concerns eluded her as she unlocked the door and withdrew, without apology, a small bottle of Stolichnaya.

Some shards of ice still floated in a Styrofoam bucket set atop the bar; these she scooped into a clean glass and cracked the bottle's seal. Vodka swirled among the ice chips like liquid crystal. She gazed into its depths as one might into a beautiful, clear lake.

The first sip burned her throat, a cold flame. The second made the edges of her brain blur just enough to feel like comfort. She rushed headlong toward that solace, craved the way outlines softened and grew indistinct. The third sip melted into the fourth, the fifth, a long draught that drained the glass; what remained of the ice chips numbed her molars.

Vera sat on the bed. A pleasant dizziness traveled the length of her muscles, spun in the top of her head. For the first time since their arrival, the books were mute, their low vibration silenced at last. Their brightness, too, had faded, their hues no more radiant than the florid drapery or the painting of parrots that hung above the bed.

Secure now in her mastery of the books, Vera slipped back into the sheets, arranged the pillows so as to prop herself upright, and reached for the pile, casually, as one might pull a paperback from the supermarket racks. The stack now rested on top of the bedclothes, nestled against her hip. Her hand stretched to capture a single volume, a book of poems, published just two years ago; its title read *Erasures*.

She studied the cover, a photograph of some generic family, circa 1960, its edges scalloped, half the black-and-white image rubbed away, as if by an unseen hand, a diagonal sweep, leaving heads and torsos without legs or feet. This partially obliterated snapshot had been menacing to Vera when she'd first looked at it in Lowell's library, but now it did not strike her as extraordinary. Her eyes brushed past it as she turned the cover back. She chose a page at random and began to read:

> *I have split*
> *the web of family,*
> *spilt that milk*
> *into a ditch.*
> *I've snipped*
> *the silken cords of love,*
> *extinguished*
> *every wish.*

Impatient, Vera turned the page. She'd never cared much for poetry; the words never quite seemed to mean what they were supposed to. Setting the book aside she rose again, returning to the mini-bar; tiny bottles stood in rows like soldiers in the dim half-light of the refrigerator. She plucked another Stolichnaya. There was no more ice.

Settling back onto the heap of pillows, she scooped the novel from the bottom of the stack. It appeared too slight to be a novel, not an inch thick even with its hard cover. The title of the book was *Splinters,* and the jacket blurb touted its "daring experimentation."

A long time ago, when Brenda was about twelve and Vera was separated from Chet, they used to read novels aloud to one another. She could remember how they'd sit on the couch with a bowl of popcorn and take turns reading chapters. They'd gotten all the way through *The Fountainhead* and were nearly done with *The Catcher in the Rye* when Chet came back, and then Brenda began spending almost all her time in her room. Vera never had read the end of *The Catcher in the Rye.*

Vera took a long sip of her drink and folded back the cover; the book spread open to the dedication page. Her eyes blurred on the letters that spelled:

For my mother,
who will never know.

Splinters

a novel by

Bryn Redding

For my mother,
who will never know.

Chapter 1

She is spread on the bed like a butterfly, pinned. Her skin is yellowed by the lamplight no one has thought to douse. Her outstretched arms are thin and tense as wires, strung from her torso to the edges of the mattress. This is only the beginning.

Her hair bleeds onto the pillow, black as a poisoned lake. A warning should be posted, rough-hewn wood etched with skull and crossbones: Danger, Do Not Drink Here. Her mouth is a gash, hacked out of her bony face. On her tongue the taste of iron settles. No sound escapes.

Her naked legs are bent at the knees, sturdy twin arches of steel. No softness there. Who would you have to be to pass through those portals? A welder, perhaps, or a wrecking ball. Between the cambers sits the hole, hole that awaits the fist. No softness there.

From the frame of the bathroom door, another she watches. Shit. I can't have that. She and she. She, another she. Her and another her. Even language conspires to keep these women from what they intend to do to each other. Do I have to give them fucking names?

I like them so much better without names. *She is spread on the bed like a butterfly, pinned.* Just a she. On a bed. Pinned. No intrusion of history. If she has a name, then she has to have a mother. And what woman with a mother would do what she is about to do, with another she? And so, she must become a woman with a past, with reasons that have led her to this bed with arms of wire and steely legs.

It's so tiresome. She is on the bed, just where I want her. There's that ugly lamplight, the color of margarine. Through the open window, the thick pulse of rap shudders into the room from the street below. Who cares how she got here? She's perfect, in this moment, just as she is. The sweat that beads in her unshaved underarms, the sharp yeast smell of her unwashed cunt. Her pupils like pinholes, stars in negative.

I don't want her to have grown up somewhere, in the heartless city or the bland suburbs or a one-room, backwoods shack. I don't want her to have gone to school or to work at some job. I don't want her to have struggled with bulimia or heroin addiction or a penchant for motorcycle gangs. I don't want her to have a mother.

That will only spoil it, don't you see?

She is on the goddamned bed. From the bathroom door, another she is watching. All right, this one's name is Luce, are you satisfied? At least, she says her name is Luce, though that is not the name her mother gave her. She is not quite naked yet. She still wears a dingy slip, grayed with laundering, one strap held with a safety pin.

You see, that is how it is with names. They come with safety pins and wardrobes and a history of laundry. Luce stole this slip from a laundromat while its owner had turned her attention elsewhere. It was already gray when she stole it; the safety pin is her own touch. The safety pin is very like her, although the slip is not.

Still, she likes the feel of it against her skin, the nylon sliding over her surfaces. Almost like having a woman to hold in her sleep.

The woman on the bed is not the kind to be held, in sleep or otherwise; she is not looking for tenderness. Luce knows this, and so the slip is a kind of protective covering, a costume or armor, to keep her skin from missing a caress. There will be no caresses.

"Didja change your mind or what?" the woman on the bed growls her complaint.

Luce chuckles. "I like to take my time."

"Well, I don't like to wait." The woman on the bed digs her fingers like claws into the mattress. "I think my high is startin' to wear off."

"Oh, no, it's not, oh no." Luce adopts a singsong soothing, a parody of reassurance. "Your high is just beginning. And if it does wear off, then I know how to fix it."

She slouches over to the bed, rechecks the tautness of the leather straps that bind the black-haired woman to the mattress. She tightens the knot on the right-hand wrist until the skin surrounding it grows white.

Then she reaches for the dark cascade of hair and grabs a handful, pulls. "I thought I told you not to talk."

The black-haired woman's face relaxes. She is now in familiar territory. Her knees spread just a little wider.

Luce extinguishes the light, plunging the room into muted darkness. This is not her favorite kind of sex. She must close off some part of herself in order to inflict pain, but she can do it when the situation dictates.

An acid fog seeps through the window, fills the room. It obscures the women on the bed, makes their bodies indistinguishable from one another. Who acts, who is acted upon? It veils every sin, muffles any sound that might break free of their reluctant throats. In the end, mist swallows everything, devouring their names, obliterating history.

Chapter 2

No matter how I might wish to deny it, everyone was a child once. Crapping in our diapers. Spitting up milk. Utterly dependent, disgustingly helpless. I forget this easily.

I mean, I saw a woman just the other night. She was dressed in tight black leather—those parts of her body that were clothed, that is, which weren't many—and her hair was shaved real close to her skull. She had this tattoo of a python that wound all the way up one leg, encircling her thigh; its head disappeared beneath the narrow swatch of skirt. Silver studs and hoops dotted her pierced nose, ears, lips, eyebrows, and navel. I saw her outside the sex club, on the one night of the week designated for lesbians. Every other night of the week, it's a sex club for men, and the women complain that the floors are always sticky. A sex club is where one goes to be fucked by people who don't know your name. When I saw her waiting, smoking, outside the club on Santa Monica Boulevard, I had to remind myself that *this woman was a child once.*

But then I thought, *maybe not.* Why do we assume a continuity of persona? An uninterrupted progression of selfhood, moving like a freight train, car after car after car, from birth to death? Perhaps it's just our names that hold together the disparate collection of identities we call a lifetime. Then what if we change our names? The train jumps the track.

Maybe it's a flimsy premise that I introduce here. Still, I need it if I am to get where I am going, so despite its theoretical pitfalls I persist: *No matter how much I might wish to deny it, everyone was a child once.*

Certainly she is no exception, although which *she* I mean, I'll leave to you to figure out. You, who have such a knack for figuring things out. Who will struggle tirelessly with this narrative, determined to wrest meaning from it, even if you have to impose that meaning, even if you have to make it up.

When she was a child, someone used to read to her. Not her mother, certainly not her mother, but someone. This child, this she, had a favorite story, one to which she never grew tired of listening, one she played out again and again in her fantasies.

It was an Andersen fairy tale. "The Snow Queen." I'm not going to tell you the whole story, but I will tell you her favorite part. Some demons devised a huge, glittering mirror with the ingenious feature that it would reflect the worst in anyone who looked at it. They decided to fly it up to heaven and shove it in God's face. But on the way up, the clumsy demons dropped it and the mirror fell to earth, where it shattered in a billion pieces that scattered throughout the world.

The bigger pieces got snatched up right away; people fashioned them into eyeglasses or windowpanes, with predictable consequences. Complacent men grew discontent, beautiful women were revealed as harridans, once-kind souls turned sour and mean. But there was more.

For centuries, the wind continued to blow invisible shards, splinters from the demons' mirror. If you were struck by a tiny piece, in the cheek, say, or the finger or the eye, you could never get it out. The splinter would pass right through the tissue, penetrate the veins, hop a ride on the blood highway, expressway to the heart. Once there, the sliver lodged deep in the muscle, creating an infinitesimal prick of pain with every pulse. And every sensitivity was filtered through its prism.

This happens in the story, to a boy named Kay. But she didn't care about him. Do I even need to tell you why she loved this story? Why she never got enough of it? Do I need to explain that this child became convinced she carried such a splinter, a fragment of the demons' glass, irretrievably stuck inside her own small heart?

Chapter 3

When she was eight years old, her mother came to sit at the side of her bed one night. Actually she wasn't in bed; she was on the living-room couch, which had been piled with pillows and blankets because she had been sick with flu, kept home from school all week. Her mother sat on the narrow edge of the couch and said, "Honey, I need you to help me."

Her mother's eyes were red-rimmed and teary, her words thick with urgency. "I need you to get up, sweetie, and put on a coat. I need you to go outside to the car for just a minute." The entreaty was propelled by an odd mixture of cajoling and matter-of-factness.

She didn't question her mother, didn't protest that she had a sore throat and it was cold outside, and snowy. She hauled herself up from the rumpled pallet, took the coat her mother extended, and buttoned it on over her pajamas. She pulled on her snow boots, too, over her bare feet, without even being reminded.

Her mother walked her to the door and delivered her instructions. "I want you to go out to the car and open up the ashtray in the front seat. I want you to look at all the cigarette butts in the ashtray and see if there are any that have lipstick on the ends. Do you know what I mean?"

She nodded solemnly. Her mother always left deep crimson stains on the filters of her Marlboros. She pushed at the storm door and stepped out onto the back porch. The steps were slippery, fresh snow covering a layer of ice. The air was chilled; she could see her breath in little puffs in front of her. Her mother stood in the doorway behind her.

Painstakingly she crossed the yard and yanked open the door to the old Buick, sliding across the cold vinyl of the front seat. She opened the ashtray and inhaled the stale bitter smell it gave off. It was dark inside the car, but she knew how to turn on the overhead light. She slid the ashtray all the way out of its cavity in the dash.

Holding it up under the light, she pulled the metal shell close to her face. She pawed through the ashes and butts, examined each one with the gravity and concentration of a research scientist. Her careful inspection yielded three with orangey pink smeared on the ends, a color she had never seen her mother wear. She wasn't sure what she was supposed to do with them, if she should bring them inside with her or leave them in the car.

Just then another car pulled up next to the house. She hastily clicked off the map light and crouched low on the seat. Her father stepped out of the other car, laughing to someone in the driver's seat. She noticed her mother quickly move away from the door and close it. Not seeing his daughter crouched on the front seat of his car, her father lurched up the steps, fumbling for his keys, cursing. The other car drove away, too fast, its wheels spinning on the icy street. Her father wrenched the door open and entered the house, slamming the door behind him.

She wasn't sure what to do then. Although her mother hadn't specifically said so, this seemed like a secret. How was she supposed to explain what she had been doing outside in the car in her pajamas, with her fingers dirty and smelling like the ashtray? It was very cold out, despite her coat and boots; she was wearing no hat or mittens. She fitted the ashtray back into its holder and brushed off her fingers, waiting for her mother to come to get her. She stuck her hands in her armpits and curled up in a tight ball on the front seat.

From inside the house she could hear the sound of an argument in progress. Well, of course her mother couldn't come out to get her during a fight. Through the kitchen window she could see the gestures of dinner being served up and eaten, the table being cleared, and then she heard more arguing.

She wanted to cry but she set her chin firmly and refused. Her nose was running, though, and she wiped it on the back of her coat sleeve. The coarse wool was rough on her reddened cheek. Finally she coiled herself even smaller on the car seat and drifted into a fevered sleep.

It was after midnight when her mother crept out to the car and, telling her to be very quiet, led her back into the house. Ratcheted snores filled the living room. Her father was asleep on the couch, on top of her favorite pillow and her Raggedy-Ann doll.

Her mother led her to bed, and just as she crawled under the covers she heard her mother's insistent whisper. "What did you find?" the woman demanded to know.

Chapter 4

Back where we started. But not quite.

Two she's lie spent on the bed. Everything that was going to happen has happened. It is a different moment now, a new chapter, a new scene. Time has jumped the tracks, continuity is broken.

You have no choice but to accept these fragments. You have to take what I give you. There is no more.

Still, you are not entirely powerless. You can always fill in the blanks, make it up in your own mind. You do it all the time: inventing an excuse for someone's inexplicable behavior, fantasizing about what the future holds, fabricating a history you don't in fact remember, assembling a persona you think the situation might require.

So don't let my lapses deter you. Take some time to imagine what these two she's have done in your absence, what kinds of smells erupted in the room, how the air must have been charged with urgency and desperation. Recall those details that made you feel good the first time you read them: the leather restraints, perhaps, the hair like a poisoned lake. Forget the parts you didn't like: the gray slip, the allusions to drug use. Or maybe those were your favorite things. I can't know. I only know that you are making a fiction of my fiction. That you are more than happy to fill in whatever I have left unsaid. Just like you've always been.

Two she's lie spent on the bed. In the aftermath of sweat and gurgled sound, they have forgotten everything that led them to this room, histories both recent and ancient. It's something like relief, but it's only temporary. The blankness in their brains is neurological, a circuit overload. In another moment it will all return, swamping that clear, empty space, deluging it with stories, identities, names, everything they were eager to escape.

When that happens, a heaviness will settle over them. They will have to decide what to do next. One she will lift her head and grumble, "Could you close that window? I hate the fucking cold," but she will not say why. Maybe she won't even think of why. One will have to decide if she should shoot more drugs or just let herself crash. Perhaps one will be hungry, or will feel like talking, and be frustrated that the other does not share these urges. One will have to determine whether to stay the night or slip back into the layers of the world, the everyday armor, and slink back out into the dark. Once, a few hours ago, it seemed so simple, every impulse leading to a single act, the breadth of existence reduced to a finite point, but already the point is dissolving, dispersing into a bewildering universe of possibility. Dread returns.

In what some like to call "real life," these two she's would never see one another again. One would hoist herself from the mattress, retrieve her drugs and her works and disappear into the fog-obliterated streets; the other would curl on the dampened sheets and think of nothing.

I can't let that happen, though. I need these two, we need them, for without them there would be just you and me.

So one of the she's will have to say, "You can stay if you want," so the other can shrug and murmur, "That's cool." What they do then is up to you: close the window, get high again, whip up a skillet of scrambled eggs. It's of no interest to me.

Except one thing they don't do, one thing they definitely don't do, is exchange histories. That I know for sure.

And I know this too. Sometime later in the night, when the fog has grown so thick that it seems that morning is both nearer and more distant than it really is, one she will have a nightmare. It will detonate her sleep like a Molotov cocktail, push adrenaline through her system until it seems her heart will burst. Her scream will wake the other. The dreamer will rise from the bed to pace in the dim gray light of the room, until her hands no longer tremble and her breath is rhythmic once again.

Still, no matter how she is cajoled, that night or later, in the morning, she will not, will not tell her dream.

Chapter 5

I know the way your mind works.

You think that because I say "I," I am revealing myself to you. You assume that the first person is personal. You believe you know something about me. This is how you get your power. You feel free to pass judgments; you decide that I'm tough or smart, wounded or seriously disturbed.

This is how Freud ruined literature. Once people read for pleasure or pain, for escape or release; they gave themselves to the story, drank it in and were satisfied. Once we experienced, now we analyze, dissecting every motivation as if there lurked within a grain of knowable truth, hidden but palpable. As if our brains were even capable of understanding. Once we perceived with our senses. Now even art becomes fodder for cheap speculation.

You think you can tell who I am just by taking these words into your brain. You imagine you've been inside me, probed the private reaches of my interior, fucked me while I willingly spread myself for you. You bask in the afterglow, secure in our intimacy.

You're so naive, it's pathetic. It never even occurs to you that I might be putting you on. Everything you see here—can you be sure it's not just a disguise? You believe you have watched me come, but how do you know I'm not faking?

Let's say you meet a woman. You sleep with her, she tells you her name is Luce. How can you be certain that it's true? How can you trust that it's not just a name she made up, or borrowed for the night? Worse yet, what if she's chosen it just because you're sure to be susceptible to such a name, find it seductive, exotic, mystical, whatever you might be looking for on that particular night?

Still, it's all you've got, so you speak it again and again, "Luce, Luce," making a kind of music with it in the dark, willing it into truth. She smiles and lets you do it, never tells you you're a fool. But no matter how you croon this name, or with what sweetness, she refuses to tell you her history, refuses to tell you her dreams.

So you start to read between the lines, interpreting each gesture, construing her most casual remarks. You invest them with meaning, your meaning, insisting it is hers. This is how you try to gain control. You imagine you can see what she has not intended to reveal. You think you understand her in a way she does not even know herself.

She tells you she was never a child, but you know better. You believe you can see into her past; you conjure visions of a chubby girl in a red snowsuit. She becomes your canvas, your conceit. The more you invent, the more you love her, feel yourself opened to her, exposed and penetrable. This too is an arresting fiction.

In this way, Luce and I are the same. You take comfort in the power relationship you have with me. You enjoy your role as the trenchant spectator, interpreter, and analyst. You imagine you can see what I have not intended to reveal. You think you're safe, hiding behind these pages. But they're only paper, after all.

Which of us is really vulnerable here?

Chapter 6

Next thing you know, it's morning. A caustic sun banishes the fog, elbows its way along the clotted boulevards and into the squalid room where two she's sleep. Rays pierce the grimy windows, force the two from their heavy slumber. One submits willingly, stretching her arms wide, turning to meet the day, while the other burrows her face in the pillow, attempting to tunnel deeper underground.

The sun is persistent, though; one might even say relentless. It has made of the first she an unwitting accomplice. She has risen from the mattress and now roams about the room, so that it is not only darkness that has vanished, but also quiet. The recumbent she clutches her black hair with both hands; the light is a hundred augers drilling into the pores of her flesh, and the sound thumps at her temples like a rubber mallet.

The act of moving from the horizontal to the vertical plane is, for her, a torturous process of reestablishing connection to her muscles and bones. That's one of the reasons she gets high, to leave the body behind, and it's always a letdown to realize she still needs it. Thus far the old skeleton continues to cooperate, to suffer her abuses without significant retaliation, but she waits for the day when the body at last refuses and she'll be stuck, twitching and supine, in some stranger's room like this, or perhaps on a plot of concrete.

Her eyes are dull as drops of lead and her mouth is a twisted grimace. Her skin has a bluish cast beneath its pale veneer. She gropes about the room until she locates the table where she left her works. She reaches for the glassine envelope. Only habit bequeaths her fingers the dexterity to unfold it.

"You're not gonna shoot up now, are you?" This is the other she, the one who has called herself Luce. This is a tone she would have never taken last night, but it is morning now and her priorities have shifted; she is no longer eager to please. "I thought you said you used it just to party."

"I could use a fucking party about now." There is a cold gleam in the leaden eyes, as her fingers shake a stream of powder into the lip of a crusted spoon.

"Go ahead. Do what you want." Luce shrugs. She has already bathed her face and rinsed her mouth with rusted water from the tap. She is prepared to let go of the night, to release the other she to her own fortunes. She has traded the dingy slip for a satin robe of lurid coral; it retains a dilapidated elegance despite its frayed cuffs and drooping hem. This item too was stolen from a thrift shop, long ago and in another country.

There comes now the awkward moment when each realizes that she does not want to be here, still in the company of the other. Last night was one thing, last night had its reasons, its purpose, its drives, but it is morning now. How stupid to allow their hasty liaison to cross the boundary of daylight. Each of them believes she is much too careful for that. It's as if someone were making them go against their own instincts.

Of course, it's true. I'm the one who overrode their wishes, forced them to stay the night. I have my own agenda. Theirs doesn't matter to me, or at least, it isn't more important to me than my own.

It is only because I insist that the two she's remain here, eyes locked across the small, scarred table. The she with the veil of black hair glowers, realizing that the other has decided she's a junkie. Defiance wars with chagrin; blood spills across her cheeks and then retreats. She flicks her cigarette lighter; the torch flares in a swirl of chemical fumes. She stares into the flame, weighing her next move. Then, with an abrupt click, she snaps shut the lid, extinguishing the flame, the metal case hot against her palm.

She slumps in her chair, the lighter gripped in her fist, the white powder waiting in the spoon. To Luce, the black-haired woman looks like a puppet whose master has let go the strings. Luce knows she has to be cautious; the last thing she needs is to end up taking care of this taut wire of a woman, one who could cut her to ribbons, or wrap around her neck and squeeze the breath out of her. Luce has done this before. Somehow, extreme as she is, she is never as extreme as the women who find her.

Chapter 7

The black-haired she is outraged to find that it nags at her, the look she sees in Luce's eyes when Luce whines, "You're not gonna shoot up now, are you?" The look that says: junkie. Fucking junkie. A cold, dismissive glare.

That the look disturbs her rankles further. What does she care what the woman who calls herself Luce thinks of her? She's been sloughing off eyes and their judgments ever since she was . . . Ever since she can remember.

And what is a junkie, anyway? Not that she is one, but even if she were? A junkie, an addict, an alkie, a pothead, a dusthead, a crackhead, a juicehead, a woman with a habit, with an attitude problem, a person with a chemical dependency, someone who just can't seem to grasp the notion of moderation, someone who carries everything to excess. The profile fits her to a T; she's always been like that, even as a . . . Even when she was younger.

But that doesn't make her a junkie, in the classic sense of someone who cannot get through the afternoon without shooting a needle full of heroin into the matrix of her blood supply. The thing that bothers her most about Luce's facile assessment is the assumption of superiority, Luce's immediate ascendance in her own mind to the position of "less fucked up." In that gaze across the table she watches the planes of Luce's face round into blandness, soften into the piggish features of the self-satisfied.

Less fucked up. What an exercise in self-delusion! There is perhaps nothing that the black-haired she hates more than that kind of psychological Darwinism, a caste system of personality that elevates those who follow the rules, act polite, and never question their existence.

That this set of characteristics does not quite describe Luce does not concern her. The look that passes from Luce's eyes to hers will from now on define Luce in her mind. Despite her fervent intention, her cunning strategy to involve herself no further with this woman than the act of skin against skin, empty of history or motive, she is defeated. She is reinventing Luce. She, too, now creates a fiction.

Just like you. Like me.

Chapter 8

I understand that you're quite upset with me.

It's been building for a while. At least since Chapter Five. Probably it started even before that, a taste of metal in the back of your throat, a souring pool in the pit of the belly, a tightening behind the eyes.

You have expectations, and I've violated them.

You say that you read for pleasure, for relaxation and escape. To crawl between covers—not unlike our two she's—for a few hours of blessed oblivion. A respite of forgetting. Names, identities, histories wink out like dying stars, swallowed in the blackness of night. To lose yourself in a fiction.

You read to be lulled, to be soothed, seduced, really. You want me to fuck you with words until the blankness claims you. Sweet desolation.

It's flattery you seek. And comfort. You expect it. You certainly don't expect to be confronted, to have your assumptions challenged, your credulity lanced like a putrid boil.

You read to escape the mirror. But I've shoved it in your face and commanded you to look.

Now you've lost all trust in me.

You hoped I would be nice; now you lament that you never really knew me. You decide that I must be a horrible person to write this way—evil, perhaps; twisted, probably; unpleasant, certainly. You find yourself wondering what could have possibly happened to make me this way.

You think there are plenty of clues. You begin to wonder with which of the two she's I identify: the woman who calls herself Luce or the raven-haired wire of a woman who might or might not be a junkie. You have a vague memory of hearing something about me—wasn't I in an anonymous twelve-step program or something?

If you're an industrious reader, you might go back to other works that I've written—poetry, short stories—searching for the common thread, seeking to construct a profile that will make sense. But it doesn't make sense.

You don't understand why I would choose to write so brutally, and about such "unsavory" characters. Do I have a troubled sex life, that I would describe this act in such a savage and unfeeling manner? Am I just cashing in on the trend toward transgressive art?

You roll it around in your head for a while, but you tire of it quickly. Life is hard enough, you decide. You don't need this shit. If this book keeps on being abusive, you promise yourself, you'll just stop reading.

Ah. There. You've found it.

Your power, I mean. Either one of us could snuff the life out of Luce and her black-haired companion in a single gesture. If a life lived on paper goes unread, did it ever really exist?

But you have additional power; you can snuff me out too: close the book, refuse to listen to me ever again, stop playing the game. You can squeeze the breath right out of me, cold and precise as the most skillful strangler. You can sentence me to eternal silence, render me mute and still as a woman in a coma. You can do that. You can.

Now, doesn't that make you feel better?

Chapter 9

It was the summer before she turned thirteen, the summer of transition from grade school to high school. 1967. The Summer of Love.

It was the summer of riots, tanks making their slow progression down Grand River Avenue. It was the first summer she did not spend in the protective custody of her grandparents. The summer when she and her mother lived alone in the house on Rosedale.

Her mother and father had split up that spring, their marriage splintered like the flimsiest plank, stepped on once too often. Her father was gone now, his things packed in the old footlocker from his military days; the house rang with the silence of his departure.

She was relieved to be alone with her mother, soothed by the cessation of nightly arguments, the slamming of doors, the crash of dishware and bone.

During that summer, she spent her days like this: She rose late in the morning, sometimes at noon, hours after her mother had left for work. Still thick with sleep, she'd go into the kitchen, scramble some eggs, eat them with toast or biscuits covered with butter and jam, and a strong cup of Lipton tea.

The radio kept her company as she slowly turned to the tasks before her. First she'd wash and put away the dishes from last night's supper and from breakfast, wash down the counters and the stovetop. Next she'd tidy the newspapers in the living room and empty the ashtrays, wiping them clean with a wet paper towel. Then she would make the beds, her own and her mother's. These chores could take all day if she were in a certain kind of mood; on those days she'd stop her work to dance to the songs on the radio, sneak experimental puffs from her mother's Marlboros, talk for hours on the phone to her best friend.

Most days, though, by midafternoon the walls would have grown confining, and she'd be ready to venture into the world. She almost always headed for the shopping center at the end of her street, lured by both its familiarity and the variety of things to look at and to do. Often she would choose to walk the long way, going around the block to the next street, to avoid interaction with any neighbor who might speak to her, ask how her mom was doing. She wanted to pass unseen through the streets.

The shopping center was not a mall, but had three grocery stores, two drugstores, a five-and-ten, an ice cream store, the Golden Palm Beauty Salon, two tiny clothing stores—one for women, one for men—a shoe store, and a greeting card shop. She knew every centimeter; during the rest of the year this was where she came every day after school.

She would certainly visit the dime store and Blackstone's Drugs, routinely browsing the book and magazine section, the makeup counter, and the candy display, where she'd purchase her daily supply. She'd check the record racks for new singles, searching for something that had not been there just the day before. Sometimes she would linger in the fabric department or visit the caged parakeets and goldfish.

On days when there was even more time to get through, she would wander into the card shop, redolent of scented candles like stale flowers, and stand, self-conscious, next to the well-dressed grandmas buying get well or happy birthday cards. On the longest days of all, she would roam the aisles of all three grocery stores: the A & P, the Big D, and Kroger's.

Once in a while, for diversion, she would walk in the other direction from her house, heading for the Dairy Queen eight blocks away. There she'd order a hot-fudge sundae studded with chopped nuts, which she'd languidly spoon from its little waxed cardboard container as she strolled the tree-lined streets of her neighborhood.

Once a week she would go on a much longer trek to the public library, over a mile away, following the same route as the one to her grade school, where she would not be returning in the fall. The walk carried her past and beyond the old school, along Grand River Avenue in the glittering sun, her arms weighted with books.

The branch library was modern, one story, built of yellow-gray brick. The inside was air-conditioned and quiet. After depositing last week's books in the slot, she slowly circled the fiction stacks, checking for new books by favorite authors, pulling out covers and titles that intrigued. Eventually she would accumulate a hefty mound, eight or ten books, as many as she could carry. These she placed in neat piles before the librarian, back covers opened and exposed for checking out, her library card atop them all.

She would carry them home again in the deepening afternoon heat, talking to herself inside her head or singing a song from the radio. Then she'd arrive back at the house to wait for her mother to come home from work; sometimes she'd look through the afternoon paper or do the crossword puzzle.

Her mother would arrive then, appearing even thinner than the day before, arms poking out of her short-sleeved dress like naked branches in winter. Her eyes would be even more hollowed in shadow.

She would hop up from the couch to greet her, then go to the kitchen to pour a drink. A martini, on ice with a twist of lemon, which her father had taught her to mix expertly, delivered into her mother's grateful hands. Then she would start to make supper. She had a number of dishes she'd learned to cook—hamburgers, pork chops, tuna casserole, tuna melt—or she might just heat up some chicken potpies. She'd make a salad, bake or boil potatoes. She was always experimenting to come up with new dishes to tempt her mother to eat. She'd keep on mixing drinks and listen while her mother talked.

Her mother would push the meal around her plate in an effort to mollify her daughter, but food seemed foreign and pointless. Over and over her mother would ask why her father would do such a thing. And what was the matter with her, failing at marriage in this way?

She always tried to answer, turning the question in her head, spinning complex theories of human behavior that years later would continue to haunt her own relationships. She would look very serious as she tried to analyze her mother. "You're a clinger, Mom," she would say to the woman across the table who regarded her with dazed, hungry eyes.

When her mother had drunk enough and begun to cry, she would send her to bed, tucking her in, trying to lull her to sleep. Then she would clear away the supper dishes and slip behind the door to her own room.

There she turned on the radio, breaking out her stash of candy and delving into a new book. The music soothed, the sugar sedated as she lost herself in the pages of fiction.

It was the summer of "Sgt. Pepper's Lonely Hearts Club Band." It was the summer she was especially fond of sour-pineapple hard candies, bracing, eaten together with saltine crackers and a tall glass of ice water, throughout the long, hot nights.

Chapter 10

The day looms empty before them, a crevasse of hours, a great gulf of un-planned time. I make the two she's spend it together. It's not at all what they want, but they can't quite figure out a way to separate. Neither she can seem to forge a credible excuse about another engagement, a pressing er-rand, a family obligation, anything to facilitate their parting.

This depresses them. Privately, each surmises that her life must be in a sorry state if there is no better way to pass the time than in the company of the other. Both take comfort in the supposition that at any moment inspira-tion will strike, provide the perfect means by which to extricate themselves from this unwilled coupling.

Secure in this conviction, they begin by getting dressed. The black-haired she has no choice but to return to the heap of clothes discarded hastily the night before. Each item is black: the tight, faded jeans; the torn T-shirt; the leather jacket; the boots like weapons. The clothes seem damp and slightly sour from the day before; still, she slides her gaunt frame into their protec-tive grasp. There are no ablutions; her hair remains a dark tangle, her mouth unrinsed. She is ready for the day.

The one who calls herself Luce removes the coral robe and slithers into a bulky sweater, the color a bilious green that yellows her complexion. This sweater was stolen from a former roommate. The truth is, all of Luce's clothes are stolen, and never from stores where they are new. Someone has always worn them before her; just whom she might or might not know. It soothes her to wear other people's clothing, relieves her of the responsibility of choosing and of having, through her choices, to invent her own persona. She likes feeling that she is made up of bits and pieces of borrowed sensibility. The sweater is paired with purple tights strafed with several runs; these were rescued from a trash bin on the street, not exactly stealing, but not shopping either. She does run her fingers through her short auburn hair, wipes the crust of sleep from the inner corners of her eyes. Wielding lipstick, she ren-ders her mouth a thick wedge of sienna before announcing that they can go.

Their heavy soles produce an arrhythmic clatter as they descend the staircase and break into daylight. Luce dons a pair of sunglasses left behind by someone in a restaurant booth; her companion merely squints and shoves her hands inside the pockets of her jacket.

They are in Luce's neighborhood, a graffiti-scarred jumble of stucco bungalows perched precariously on palm-lined hillsides. Down the hill, the streets are crowded with squat buildings sporting signs in Spanish, Chinese, Vietnamese. The morning is lively with commerce; men congregate in the doorway of an auto parts store while women drag reluctant children through the entrance of a hair salon. The parking lot of the Chinese grocery is jammed; idling cars spew exhaust into the fetid air.

Luce leads the other she to an outdoor food stand; its sign offers Pastrami Tacos Burgers. A few rusted metal chairs and tables lean dispiritedly on the sidewalk. The black-haired woman orders only coffee, disdaining Luce's hearty endorsements for the "breakfast burrito," a bean-and-egg conglomeration that Luce drenches in *salsa verde* and downs in a few ravenous bites.

"You oughta get some protein." Luce dispenses this unsolicited advice offhandedly, in a manner that suggests, "I don't really care if you do or not."

"Don't." The black-haired she glowers. "Don't fucking mother me." Her body has snapped to attention, rigid as a switchblade pressed into service.

"Don't worry." Luce crumples the paper wrapper from her breakfast and discards it in a wire bin. She has to fight the desire to strike back, to kick the aging chair out from underneath the other so she sprawls on the pavement, to throw steaming, bitter coffee in her face. Luce figures she could just break into a run, intercept the bus flying down Sunset, and board it, bound for anywhere, escape the need for ersatz explanations, ritual good-byes.

Luce does none of these things; I won't let her. She stands. The black-haired she stands too, spitting a mouthful of coffee grounds onto the sidewalk in a great glob. They are at an impasse.

Without speaking, they begin to amble up the block. Passing a *panaderia*, the black-haired woman dashes in, returns with three sugar-dusted pastries that she eats from a napkin while Luce resists the urge to lecture. Instead she asks herself, "What would you expect a junkie to eat for breakfast?"

Desire has evaporated like last night's fog, burned off by the daylight, and in its place a kind of repulsion has taken hold, as powerful as lust. Disgust with the other, and with herself for being with the other, encircles each of them like coils of a rope, binding them more tightly than love ever could.

Chapter 11

I once knew a woman who, owing to a disability and through no fault of her own, had only minimal control of her sphincter muscles. As a consequence, her underwear was frequently riddled with shit. Sometimes, too, her bedsheets.

I know this, but not because the afflicted woman chose to share the information with me. She told no one but her lover. I can almost picture her halting confession, the blush of shame, the hushed voice, eyes pleading for acceptance. The lover's whispered reassurances.

The lover told a friend, who was my lover at the time. Perhaps in the spirit of complaint, "See what I have to put up with?" No doubt my lover had complaints of her own, and who knows how one set of allegations stacked up against the other?

By the time it was told to me, the woman's secret had acquired the aura of gossip, a thrall of horror edged with amusement, an irresistible naughtiness. I could never again look at the woman without a feeling of particular smugness. I knew something about her, and she was helpless before my knowledge. Information, after all, is power.

I wonder now at the lover, at someone who would trade in this currency of secrets. Was this, to her, an act of power, a weapon of superiority, irrefutable proof that she was "less fucked up?" A means to discredit the woman whom she, perhaps, hated just as much as she loved? Or was it that the burden of intimacy fell too heavily on her, that she could not bear the weight of this secret alone? So that she was compelled to share it, and with people who did not have the same feelings for the woman that, at least, the lover claimed to? People who would be sure to pass it on until the power of the secret had been rubbed away like chalk on a blackboard, the intimacy dispersing in the air like white dust, and she was safe again?

Chapter 12

Once upon a time, as all the old stories begin, there were two little girls.

One child was pale as ice, translucent, brittle, her eyes opaque as frozen water. Quiescent and mute. Everybody thought she was so good.

The other child was furious. Messy, squalling, criminal, fierce. Her yowling mouth an unhealed scar in her dirty face. No one liked to think about her; it was easier to pretend that she did not exist.

The girls lived in the same house, but they occupied different regions. Perhaps one held a dim awareness of the other, hearing the stomp of footfalls on the ceiling or muffled weeping from a distant room; still, their paths did not cross.

It was an exploding house they lived in, given to eruptions without warning and never-ending cataclysm. Screams in the night, the thump of bodies falling down the basement stairs, step after step after step. A haunted house, then. Wired with dynamite.

Each detonation sent the good girl deeper into hiding, creeping inside the freezer chest at the bottom of the house to lie beside the gelid carcasses, the rock-hard vegetables in their plastic shrouds, silent, without breath. Nested there, her skin would turn silver as frost in moonlight, and her brain would empty. Her heartbeat slowed, the ictus languid and moribund. This was peace. No one came to look for her.

The blasts of the exploding house, however, sent the other girl into the streets, slipping through the cracked pane of her bedroom window, where the night waited to claim her. She stole everything she could from the darkness; she was the most cunning of thieves. She became darkness. She was speed and motion, havoc, and in the streets she set herself aflame, night after night, burning brighter than the house she had escaped. Throwing up sparks into the trees, blackening the weeds of the unmown lawn.

Eventually a neighbor would come by, a neighbor or a stranger who would force her back into the house. Ignoring the seared skin that hung in strips from the frame of her bones, they'd say, "It's not safe out here for a young girl. You go on home." Home to the house where the floors shuddered and walls snatched the breath from the air. House that could not contain her.

Uneasy roommates, invisible to one another, poised at either end of the abyss. Two little girls. Two she's.

You may, of course, be tempted to assume that this is a parable of our two she's. This would be a serious mistake, a folly, a detour that would leave you hopelessly lost, a path from which there could be no return.

These two little girls have their own stories to tell. They're not replicas, not miniature versions of anyone. They did not grow up to be someone who calls herself Luce and someone who might or might not be a junkie.

They didn't grow up at all.

They still live in the house, still occupy that territory, that terrain both unsettled and fixed. One cradles her head against frost in the deep freeze, concealed and unmissed. One incinerates herself in the front yard, blazing for all to see.

Together they are perfect symmetry. Two girls in an exploding house.

Chapter 13

So, how do these women earn a living?

That's what you want to know.

You're persistent; I'll give you that. No matter how I try to elude them, you keep asserting your demands for story, your hunger for the classic elements of fiction: character, plot, conflict—all the skills my students, bent earnestly over their note pads, struggle to attain. I've tried telling them it's worthless, atavistic crap, obsolete and inappropriate to the conditions of contemporary life, but they don't believe me. And why would they, because there you are, the audience, clamoring for just these elements, proving me wrong, wrong, wrong.

I'm not insensitive to your needs. I try to think of what will make you happy, short of telling you an outright lie. Although I don't have much faith in truth—you know, as a concept—certain kinds of lies do seem to me immoral. Spinning a fiction that lulls you with a false sense of safety, a counterfeit hope, would seem like that kind of lie.

Still, I try to think of what will make you happy. I do care about that, despite what you assume. In fact, I want desperately to make you happy, but first I have to make you suffer. Just a little. If you don't suffer first, how will you know for sure that it was I who restored you to happiness? You might not know for sure, and that's a risk I can't afford to take.

How do the two she's earn a living?

I'll give you choices:

The woman who calls herself Luce cleans office buildings at night. She likes the hours, the solitary nature of the work. She likes the icy gleam of fluorescent bulbs in a darkened building, the harsh fumes of the cleaning solvents. She likes stealing random office supplies: a box of fresh, unsharpened pencils, a roll of scotch tape. She could never *work* in an office, never work at the *business* of an office, but she finds it soothing to roam about in the empty hull of an office once business has ceased for the night.

The black-haired she was kept for many years by a wealthy old queen who found it amusing to have a constant companion to whom he could always feel superior. He expected little of her besides that, and she did the job well. The old queen died a few months ago, leaving her a little settlement, though not, sadly, the tastefully appointed house in the Hollywood Hills. If she's careful, she can stretch her inheritance to last for a few years. Or she can blow it all at once on something stupid. She hasn't decided yet. She's keeping her options open.

Or:

The woman who calls herself Luce reads tarot cards in one of those ratty storefronts on Vermont. She doesn't really know a thing about the cards and their interpretation, but then, neither do most of the desperate people who seek her services. Her philosophy is this: If you tell people that good things will happen to them, they become suspicious; if you predict calamity, they trust you fully. If, through her readings, she leads her customers to expect miracles (windfalls, new love, their health restored) then no matter what small good fortune might actually befall them, they are inevitably disappointed. If, however, she encourages them to anticipate the worst (hidden enemies, infidelity, *le morte*), then they are likely to be relieved by whatever events do transpire in their lives, and return to see her again and again.

The black-haired she demands spare change at the end of a downtown freeway ramp, accosting commuters who must wait for the traffic light to change. With the sprawl of high-rise buildings as her backdrop, she carries a Styrofoam cup scavenged from a dumpster and a hand-lettered sign that reads Ten month old babye. Needs food. Help. Please. Thank you. God bles. On a good day she can pull in twenty-five to thirty dollars just from morning and evening rush hours—better than an eight-hour shift at Taco Bell.

Or:

Luce works the counter at a West Hollywood coffeehouse, a place called Bad Beans. Maybe you know it—it's been featured in several glossy spreads on "the new coffeehouse phenomenon." Nights, from 9:00 until 2:00 in the morning, she dishes up industrial strength espresso and fat wedges of flavorless cake to the would-be intellectuals who smoke and flirt and pretend to read French philosophers.

The black-haired woman plays the horses, Santa Anita, Hollywood Park, sometimes all the way to Del Mar when she can get a ride. The old-timers want to know her system. She tells them, "Raw impulse. Sheer nerve. A willingness to lose everything."

Or:

. . . plays bass in a rock band called Little Girls from Hell.

. . . works at a video store.

. . . is a minor celebrity in hard-core porn.

. . . pumps gas.

. . . pens a column for the alternative weekly.

. . . is a hired assassin.

Fill in the blank.

I can tell you some things they don't do, too.

Neither of the two she's has worked as a dental technician, a paralegal, or a candy striper. They're not models or cocktail waitresses or hairdressers. They're not massage therapists, MBAs, MFCCs. They have never been employed as librarians or airline stewardesses. They're not salesgirls. The two she's have never earned their living as marketing directors or political appointees. They're not women priests or rabbis. No one has ever paid them to be research physicists or highway workers or astronauts. You won't find them working as chefs or veterinarians or merchant marines.

You're right, you're right; I don't know when to quit. I suppose I would have made you perfectly happy if I'd just answered the question, but don't you see? That's the kind of lie I was talking about, the easy answer that allows you to say, "Okay, I've got it now. I know these women."

But you don't, that's the point. You don't know them. You don't know them at all.

Chapter 14

The details of my life are so mundane.

Not at all exotic, not like the two she's. No one would ever write a novel of *my* life.

I meet some of you, sometimes, crowding up to me after a reading or at a book signing, clutching a copy of one of my books and a pen, wanting to add me to your collection. I see the disappointment in your eyes: I am not what you expect. I do not look like steel wire, like a knife blade or a poisoned lake. I do not feed your fantasies: I am too real.

A little overweight. A few wrinkles. My hair is no outrageous color but the same dull gold it's always been, now stitched through with a few strands of silver.

My name is Bryn. That is not the name my mother gave me, but then, I am not the person my mother intended me to be. She is not the person I intended her to be, either. See? Symmetry.

There, I've admitted it: I was a child once. I have a mother. I have a history. But really, that's so tedious, isn't it? I have spent my life trying to escape my history. And who will say that I did not succeed?

I have a lover. That probably surprises you. Certainly the unstable women in my fiction cannot sustain a stable relationship.

At the very moment I am writing this, my lover is in the next room watching "Oprah." Really. In a little while, she will read this and complain, "Don't put that in; people will think I do it all the time." She doesn't, though. Really. Just today.

We own a house. I pay my bills on time. I vote. I like to cook and garden. Really. Very mundane. Not the stuff of fiction.

It is true. I am a member of an anonymous twelve-step program. Three, actually. *God grant me the serenity....* I won't tell you which three, but as far as I can remember, I have never stuck a needle full of anything into my veins. Although I am certain I have lied about that, telling people that I have; I thought it would make me seem more dangerous. As if I needed to be any more dangerous.

Or perhaps I thought that would be a more acceptable kind of danger. A decoy, if you will.

I used to do that all the time. Lie. It was never to make myself seem better. I always lied to make myself seem worse. Or, *even* worse. One can get power out of being "more fucked up" just as surely as from being "less fucked up."

What have *I* done for money? I've waitressed. Been a typesetter. Written grants. Modeled for art students. For many years of my life I was paid—well, barely—to pretend to be somebody else, which is to say, I was an actress. Not a great one. A good one, maybe. I could never quite obliterate myself enough to be a great one; I wonder whether I'd be any better at it now. Although some might say that fiction writing is just the same, pretending to be somebody else. The ultimate disguise.

I'm tired of all that, though. I want to step out from behind the veils. That's why I want to talk to you. Why I want you not to be fooled.

But what can you trust? I've told you so many different things, shown you so many different faces.

I'll promise you this at least: Even when I lie to you, it's real.

Chapter 15

The two she's take their time making their way west along Sunset. It is Saturday and they can afford to be leisurely; nothing and no one awaits them. The sun gleams overhead, indifferent, unforgiving. The black-haired she has removed her leather jacket and slung it over one shoulder; the woman who calls herself Luce perspires inside her chartreuse sweater. The beige sky enfolds them like a cupped hand.

The black-haired she wrestles a joint from her jacket pocket and fires it up, sucking the sweet fumes deep into her throat. She smokes it down to a nub and never offers Luce a hit.

Luce pretends not to notice. She leads the way, pokes her nose against windows, investigates the crumbling retail establishments that line the boulevard. She exhibits the same droll curiosity in the hardware store as she does in the botanica and the thrift shop, but it is only from the latter that she emerges with a pilfered men's dress shirt stuffed beneath her baggy sweater.

After they've walked another block, she pulls it from its hiding place, shaking out the wrinkles and admiring its starched whiteness. "It's starting to get hot," she says, by way of explanation. "I need to find a place to change."

Without a word, the black-haired she takes her elbow, guides her down a side street and into a narrow alley, unseen from the street. She pushes Luce against a stucco wall, yanks the hem of her sweater and pulls it over her head, exposing her large white breasts to the glare of the sun and the houses on the overlooking hillside. Luce struggles to free her arms from the sweater, lets it drop to the dirt.

For a moment the two she's look at each other. They have felt no desire for one another since the previous night, so unremembered that it might have been years ago instead of hours; they have in fact been steeped in the opposite of desire all morning, but this unexpected circumstance inspires possibility. The traffic of Sunset rumbles, just yards away. The windows of apartments cast a hundred eyes upon their alley: Anyone could see. Their antipathy for one another curdles into lust.

The black-haired she hooks her fingers in the waistband of Luce's tights and slowly pulls, down, until Luce's body is bare to the knees, which are abruptly purple. The black-haired she insinuates a hand between the naked thighs; the hand begins to flex and twist.

Luce arches her hips forward, spreads her legs as widely as she can, bound as they are by the leggings. The sun reddens her bare skin; she can feel the scrape of stucco at her back. The black-haired she proves to be surprisingly adept, her fingers thrusting, knuckles probing, seeming to fondle all of Luce's slippery surfaces. The black-haired she does not kiss her—they have never kissed—but instead slips a finger from her free hand into Luce's mouth, the skin still sweet from the sugary pastries, and does not cry out when Luce's teeth sink in.

Luce begins to shudder and buck; she lifts up onto her toes, drawing the hand of the black-haired she deeper into her. She sucks at the finger furiously; she could draw blood, but she refrains. At last she cries out, a screech like the sound of a wild bird caught in the jaws of a cat; her heels return to earth, hips tilt back to rest against the wall.

She stares into the eyes of the black-haired she, eyes blue as a cold ocean. Something is swimming there, but Luce does not know what it might be. The black-haired she withdraws her fist from the folds of Luce's vulva; she raises the hand to her own lips and, carefully inserting each finger, licks them clean. She does this with just a ghost of a smile.

With unexpected gallantry, the black-haired she bends to retrieve the fallen sweater from the pavement, but Luce is sliding into the shirt, which has been clutched, forgotten all this time, in her left hand. As she moves to fasten the buttons over her breasts, she glances up. From a second-story window, an old man with a stiff mustache regards the two she's with undisguised fascination.

Luce takes her time pulling up her tights, stretching them against her thighs and over her ass. She makes sure the man is still watching as she knots the chartreuse sweater around her waist.

She is utterly satisfied; she knows the old gentleman will not be able to forget what he has seen in the alley, will continue to think about it all day. He will make it part of his fiction, a story he tells himself to fall asleep; perhaps he will carry it with him through whatever remains of his life, an image more powerful than dreams.

Chapter 16

The two she's come to me in a dream. They storm the room; they are furious, blowing open doors and busting windows. They seem to carry with them light—a candle, a torch, a searchlight—I cannot identify its source.

They seem to be shouting my name: Bryn, Bryn. The sound crashes like cymbals in an overture. There are other things too, but I can't make them out, shouted syllables mere bursts of noise.

The woman who calls herself Luce carries a coil of rough rope. She straps me to the bed, looping the binding around each of my ankles and wrists, tightening the grips until the fibers bite my skin. She is thorough and quick, and I am trussed before I can even think to protest.

The black-haired she straddles my chest, her steely legs clamped like stays around my rib cage, squeezing. Her mouth opens wide above my face, the dark entrance to hell. Her breath is a hot, foul wind at my nose; her words splatter like chunks against my hair.

She spews out: "You think you're hot shit, don't you? You think you made us up, that we belong to you, that you can do whatever you want to us?"

Luce has taken the position above my head, seated on the rise of my pillow, forcing my skull into the V of her legs. She wears no underwear; there is a sour odor between her thighs, yogurt left too long in the sun. She has grabbed hold of my eyelids, yanking them open, insisting that I see the black-haired woman perched like an enormous spider on my chest.

The black widow is still shrieking: "You did not invent us. You're not in control here, no matter what you think."

She brandishes the syringe; it is full of blood. The needle glints in the light above my head, the point sharp and dazzling. "Starting now," she snarls, "things are gonna change around here. You're gonna do what we say. Without us, you're nothing, and it's time you showed the proper respect."

Luce punctuates the other she's remarks with a stinging slap on each of my cheeks. I don't mind that so much. It's just that her companion keeps poking her index finger into my sternum, which I mind a lot and which draws a harsh rattle from my lungs.

The black-haired she leans closer, her eyelashes nearly entangling with my own. "So whaddaya say? Are you gonna save yourself?" A stream of spittle drips from her mouth into mine, burns against my gums.

There are so many things I don't understand. Do they want me to stop writing about them altogether, or only to portray them in a more flattering light? Do they want me to make them seem better, or to make them seem worse? To lie more, or to tell more truth?

I haven't freighted them with histories, haven't betrayed their secrets. Or is it by this omission that they feel betrayed? I want to make them happy, but there are things I don't understand. My tongue seems to have swollen to fill the whole basin of my mouth. Try as I might to force a question out, no sound escapes my throat.

My silence seems to satisfy. With unexpected tenderness, the black-haired she plunges the hypodermic into my vagina. The warm blood enters me, red as tomato soup. The murky fluid is teeming with life; spirochetes tumble slowly upward, snowflakes spiraling in reverse, staking their claim to my viscera.

The two she's rise from my bed and prepare to leave. The woman who calls herself Luce coos in parting, "We'll just leave you tied up here to give you time to think on what we've said." Then they are gone: the light, the noise, and all sensation. I might as well be dead. The dream is over.

Chapter 17

She was thirteen now and it was spring. The world outside the house was newly thawed, reborn, a proliferation of green beneath the warming sky. The lilac bush was purpling against the house next door, and just yesterday she had noticed lily of the valley blooming in back of the garage.

Inside the house, time was moving backward. The temperature was dropping; blossoms were retreating back into shriveled buds, sunlight fading into gray. Her father had returned to the house on Rosedale.

She was huddled in a corner of her room. Crouched on the floor, pressed against the bookcase. Through the window just above her head, the scent of lilacs drifted in, mocking the bare branches and frozen ground of the interior. Clutched in her hand was a book—*Soul on Ice*—which she pretended to read, eyes scanning the printed characters again and again, her brain empty of their meaning.

The door to her bedroom was closed. There was no lock. Still, it was purposefully shut. She tried to imagine it would be some kind of barrier.

Beyond the closed door of the bedroom, shouts were escalating. Accusations were being hurled, threats were levied. She wanted not to listen, but she could not will herself deaf, so instead she tried to hear the commotion as pure noise, discordant music, jagged blasts of sound divorced from meaning, fractured syllables hurtling through space.

It was a familiar tune, and it produced in her a familiar terror. For a while this music had not been heard in the house on Rosedale and she had tried to forget it. Except, she could never really forget it; its melody was in her cells, her nerves attuned to every nuance of its orchestration. Now time was moving backward. The music had returned, and she had the strange sensation of time collapsing on itself, of being funneled back into a past she'd thought she was done living through.

The tempo was accelerating. Her heart kept time. The volume grew deafening, rattled the closed door on its hinges. She crouched lower to the floor, burrowing nearer to the bookcase as if to crawl inside. Her eyes burned into the open pages before her, pleading with the printed words for sanctuary, but they rebuffed her. Her eyes were no match for her ears.

Then a new sound was introduced, a stark percussion she had never heard before yet which was unmistakable, as if she had been waiting for it all her life. A sound that was the end of all sound.

The gunshot tore the air, rupturing both the music that preceded it and the silence that dropped like a curtain after it sounded. Silence. Beyond the door all was silence. Time stopped.

Inside her room, too, everything froze. The quiet stretched as wide as time itself. She no longer knew who she would be, what kind of world waited on the other side of the door.

Despite this unknowing, she had only one thought resounding in her head, as clear and unambivalent as the drum of the bullet blasting from her father's gun: "I don't care which one it is," she told herself, and meant it. "At least it will be over."

But it was not over, not then, not for a long time, not ever. She never learned which one had fired the gun, or why. She knew only that the silence had at last dissolved once more into everyday music, a music that denied the percussive boom and its potency. Time returned to its holding pattern, the minutes falling like rain into a stream of hours, a river of time that flowed nowhere at all.

• • •

Years later, she will try to get her mother to recall this story. Her father will be gone again, presumably for good; she will assume that it is safe now to talk about such things. Her mother will insist it is nothing but a vile fiction, yet another punishment her daughter is visiting upon her. She will lead her mother to the kitchen, patiently showing the hole embedded in the cabinet, still visible under layers of paint.

Her mother will have no alternate explanation, will merely blink before the evidence, her face empty of memory. Her mother will say: "If that's the story you tell yourself, you must be a very unhappy person."

She will hear these words, spit like bullets from between her mother's lips, and feel again the waters of time close all around her, pulling her limbs, sucking her breath. It will drag her under.

Chapter 18

I never meant for it to be like this.

In the beginning, there were just two she's, brought together by casual impulse. Two she's in a room, in lamplight. One tied to the mattress, the other soon to join her there. There was fog, to fill up all the empty space between them.

It could have been any two she's. Two debutantes. Two aging nuns. Two escaped convicts. Two Polish seamstresses. They might have been pretty and cheerful, or wealthy and selfish, or courageous and noble. They could have been blond or hunchbacked or sculpted by reconstructive surgery.

I could have put them on a farm or astride Harleys or perched on leatherette stools at the nail salon. There could have been a war raging outside, or a party going on downstairs. *That wasn't important to me.*

In the beginning, I was sure it would be possible to introduce you to these two she's, to let you come to know them solely by their actions. No, that's wrong. I never meant for you to know them; in fact, I wanted to prove to you that it was not possible to know them. That to *observe* is not to *know*, insofar as *to know* implies possession. The only thing that you might possibly come to know is yourself, the way even a broken mirror reflects those who gaze into its depths.

So it was against knowing, then, that I launched the two she's. Without names, without mothers, without histories. Unbound from story. Freed from the burden of interpretation.

How I envied them!

There are critical theorists who believe that we are moving toward a future in which meaning itself will be obsolete, the concepts of morality and judgment defunct. The thread of causality snapped, we will be left to spin in a world of action divorced from consequence, where continuity is no longer assumed or desired.

Perhaps this will be the end of story.

Even though I'm a writer, I hope it's true. It seems like a relief to me, who has spent a lifetime trying to escape the story that was written for me, dodging consequences like bullets. I'd gladly take my place in line behind the cobblers and the hatcheck girls, the stenographers, typesetters, boilermakers, all of us whose services are no longer required by the coming millennium.

I even thought that you might find it a welcome change as well, a respite from the well-mannered lies, the intrusive disquisitions, the thinly based assumptions in which most authors indulge. Well, that was my assumption, wasn't it? And how wrong I was! Why, I never really knew you at all, did I?

The truth is, right away it began to fall apart. Before I'd even finished scribbling the fourth paragraph, I had to produce a name for one of them, to avoid the pesky problem of *she* and *she.* A signifier, even if it was a code name and not a real one. But the trouble with signifiers is that they, well . . . *signify,* which by its very definition leads us right back to meaning. *If she has a name, then she has to have a mother,* and we're suddenly tunneling back through time, pulled farther and farther from that future without consequence.

I should have known I was in trouble, should have thrown in the towel right then, set down the pen, gone to watch "Oprah." But that was minor, kid stuff, compared to the difficulties that came next.

Because no matter how I tried to write about the she's, pieces of another story kept breaking through. Fragments of a shattered mirror. Another she with her story, a story I can neither contain nor escape.

Chapter 19

Now it is more dangerous.

The two she's have emerged from their alley, resumed their place on the sidewalk beside the mothers dragging baskets of clean laundry, bags of groceries, grimy toddlers; next to the teenage girls sporting eyeliner in black slashes like swords, waving to cars full of boys with their radios cranked loud; amongst the clusters of stoop-shouldered men, murmuring in soft accents and passing bottles of beer.

The she's proceed with their westward journey along Sunset, but their movements are slowed. They find themselves burdened, laboring under the weight of shared experience. Less than twenty-four hours after meeting, they are already saddled with history.

They carry "the first time," which would have been the only time and therefore unremarkable were it not for "the second time," which by its very cataloguing points to the possibility of a third time, a fourth, a fifth. The charge, not only of history but also of future, presses in, as if the sky and the pavement had begun a headlong rush into each other's arms, with no regard for what was sandwiched in between.

They carry now the old man's eyes as he watched from his window. They carry the slip with the safety pin, the spoon encrusted with heroin cooked brown, the residue of Mexican pastries, the stolen shirt. All this and more makes up the chain they drag. With every step another link is forged.

This is much more dangerous. This is not like them. Neither she is the type to reminisce. Both take pride in being rootless in the here and now, each moment a new present, unencumbered by the moment that preceded it, action without consequence.

But here's the problem: Now it's all written down.

I'm the one who's done it to them, saddled them with story. Without me, who is there to draw the line between the safety pin and the old man's eyes? Who is there to say that a minute has anything to do with the one before or the one that follows? Who except the storyteller assumes continuity?

That's what has made the she's furious. That's why they come to torture me in dreams, inflicting me with a dose of my own medicine.

But it's too late. Because even if I tell them, "It's okay, you can go now. You don't have to stay together; you can part right here, in front of the Cuban bakery," they can't do it. They're bound up in story, in shared experience; these pages form a chain too strong to be broken.

I'm contrite, awed by the consequence of what I've done. And I do try to set them free. I tell them, "I don't need you anymore. It's time to go your separate ways. Go on! Scat!" But it's too late.

So they enter the Cuban bakery, take their seats at chrome-legged tables and order cups of dark, bitter espresso. They will sit here until it occurs to them to do something else. I have no idea what that will be.

I wish there were something I could say. What could I say: I'm sorry? I'll keep in touch? Don't worry be happy? Maybe I could share with them something I've learned, something wise that will resonate with them for the rest of their days.

But what have I learned? Perhaps only this: that intimacy is the assumption of knowing, that is, of possession, of creating a fiction about someone that is really all about oneself. That all intimacy is betrayal.

That's what I could tell them, but they probably already know.

And what of you and me? Have we, too, been intimate, here between the covers? And if that's true, then which of us has betrayed the other?

Enough, enough. No consequences, no recriminations. The woman who calls herself Luce is thinking of ordering ice cream, banana or mango or coconut. The black-haired she taps out a nervous rhythm with her spoon on the tabletop.

I imagine I feel their hollow, indifferent eyes at my back as I turn and walk away.

Chapter 20

Let me tell you my version of "The Snow Queen"—the story Hans Christian Andersen couldn't bring himself to tell.

Once upon a time, the Devil created a mirror. Was it really *the* Devil or just *a* devil, or was it just another crackpot inventor with a vision whose implications had not been adequately taken into account? Just another technocrat with a recipe for destruction?

Once upon a time, such questions were not raised. If someone claimed to be the Devil, we tended to believe him. Now we are more jaded, skeptical of devils and scientists alike, so accustomed to the prospect of destruction that we face it with indifference. But I digress. The "by whom" doesn't matter: A mirror was made.

And no ordinary mirror, I assure you; this one was singular. In its silvered plane the world was reflected exactly as it was, not as it was idealized to be. It showed the treachery that lurked beneath façades of beauty, the cowardice masquerading as good. When someone gazed into its depths, the mirror unveiled that person's essence, not the face they showed to others. Thus, a popular mayor was shown naked and fornicating, and the demure wife of the minister was portrayed dispensing justice to her toddler with the width of a thick belt.

It wasn't long before news of the mirror reached God's ears. Was it *the* God or just *a* god, or was it just whomever was in power at the time? Again, it doesn't matter. God decreed that the mirror must be destroyed. God had an investment in keeping certain truths hidden, in sugarcoating certain harsh realities.

So God sent down a stupendous thunderbolt that shattered the mirror with its might. God claimed it was an act of God, and thus avoided paying damages to its rightful owner. But the mirror's destruction turned out to be another idea with implications that had not been entirely thought through. Because when the glass exploded, its fragments were hurled to every corner of the earth.

Then all kinds of people had their own little slivers of mirror. Never had the potential for insight been greater. But people didn't want to see the world exactly as it was. Rather than stare into the glass and face the truth depicted there, the people made themselves go blind. God needn't have gotten so excited in the first place.

Still, this did not eliminate the problem. Aside from the larger slices of the mirror, used as interesting decorations for the blind, tiny shards were everywhere. You might mistake one for a grain of sand in your dinner, or a speck of soot in your eye, a bit of grit in the bottom of your shoe.

Once a splinter from the mirror was inside you, you could never get it out. It worked its way into the bloodstream, swam in the crimson currents until it reached the pumping island of the heart. Like a seed in earth, the splinter nested in the tissue. There it grew, multiplied like frost crystals until the heart was ice.

Once upon a time there was a she, a she with a splinter in her heart. It had come to her when she was just an infant—she didn't quite know how—and had been there for so long that she could not remember the time before her heart was pricked. With each pulse of that muscle, the shard bit deeper, but by now the organ was so frozen that she didn't feel it. And the rime that glimmered with a boreal light cleared her vision, and she saw the world exactly as it was, and not the way it was idealized to be.

She was called the Snow Queen. Was she *the* Snow Queen or just *a* Snow Queen, or was this just an epithet hurled by those who squirmed beneath her pitiless eye, her glacial heart? It doesn't matter. That is how she was signified.

Once upon a time there was another she. She and she: two she's. This second she had the misfortune to fall in love with the one who was called the Snow Queen. Now, being a sensible sort, she realized the folly of trying to love someone with a heart of ice. Still, she believed herself to be helpless before her fate. So she became determined to change the Snow Queen, to melt her frozen heart and claim her love.

The industrious she tried everything—flattery, passion, smothering, rage—to spark a fire in the Snow Queen's heart. The Snow Queen failed to thaw.

She confided her deepest and most heartfelt secrets. The Snow Queen mocked her and betrayed her confidences, spreading the wretched girl's vulnerabilities as gossip.

At last, in despair, she unleashed a torrent of tears, which pooled about the Snow Queen's feet and began to freeze into a plane of silvery glass. Taking pity on the miserable she, the Snow Queen chipped a tiny shard from the frozen pool beneath them. Reaching for the hand of the inconsolable she, the Snow Queen pricked the girl's finger, stabbing the splinter deep into the wound.

Our she had to keep from crying out, in pain and in surprise, as the sliver sunk into her flesh. But because it was the Snow Queen who had done it, and because this gesture was the most affection the Snow Queen had ever shown her, she silenced her objections. The shard made its way through layers of derma to enter her bloodstream, where it picked and clawed through arteries and veins before arriving at her heart.

Now she too began to freeze, her ventricles congealing, body temperature plummeting, her skin woven with a delicate pattern of frost. Gazing into the eyes of the Snow Queen, cold and clear as diamonds, she saw the world exactly as it was, and knew they would be bonded for all time.

And through lips numbed with cold, she whispered, "Mother."

Chapter 21

Ever since the time her father pulled her into the bathroom and taught her all about "how men make babies," ever since he'd shown her how to slide her mouth along the swollen shaft that jutted from below his navel, and squirted sticky cream against her cheek, she'd learned to hide.

Not in obvious places like closets or under furniture or in the basement, places where she was certain to be caught. She became a master of concealment, changing her shape, her size, her coloring, folding her body into spaces it was never designed to fit.

She wouldn't wait to hear his footfall on the step, the rasp of his key in the lock; she didn't try to read these sounds, to gauge the margin of safety. She simply hid as soon as she got home from school, an hour or more before her parents arrived, so that she would never again be caught off guard.

Sometimes it was her mother who would get home first, and call her name and search the rooms. It was hard to resist her mother's voice—first plaintive, turning anxious, then angry—made younger with a panicked helplessness. But resist she did, forcing herself to remain hidden, deafening herself to the lure of that voice, its needs.

Other times her father arrived first. He never said anything, appeared not to notice her absence. He would turn on the TV, mix a drink in the kitchen, settle onto the sofa and smoke. Every once in a while he would get up, walk over to a closet or a cabinet and pull its door abruptly open, as if to catch her unawares, but, finding nothing, he would casually close it again and resume his quiet drinking.

Only when her mother joined him did his search acquire vigor. Then he'd slam through the house, barking her name, peppered with threats: "Goddamn it, I've had about enough of this," and "When I find you, you're gonna be fucking sorry you were born," while her mother cajoled and menaced. Sometimes, in frustration, he would turn against her mother, and she felt a sickening guilt to hear the shouts or thuds of fists and know she was responsible.

She was never discovered. She had learned to erase all signs of entry into her chosen hiding place. She had learned to ignore cramps in her muscles, her extremities falling asleep. She had learned to be as quiet as death itself, to stifle sneezes, yawns, and belches. She had learned to choose a spot that would provide a source of oxygen.

Only once she heard the sound of her father's snores would she emerge, careful not to disclose where she had been. Her mother would find her in her room, as if she had always been there, and neither entreaties nor threats nor the infliction of punishment could persuade her to betray her hiding place.

This continued for years, until she was old enough to not come home anymore.

Even now, when she thinks of that time, the time that some might call "her childhood," what she remembers is mostly darkness. Her limbs compressed by the confines of her sanctuary. Taking shallow, soundless breaths in through her nose. The smell of scorch or mildew, plastic or wood rot, dust.

Outside, they are calling. They kick the furniture, they shriek her name. They cannot stand that she eludes them, that she exists in places they can't see. They tear the rooms apart, search the absolute parameters of their known world. They never find her.

25.

Vera

By the time Vera began the tortured process of groping toward wake-fulness, like a half-blind creature stumbling through a dark tunnel, rays of sun were already streaming through a crack in the curtains, drill-ing beneath her crusted eyelids. She could hear the housekeepers prowl-ing the halls with their vacuums and cleaning carts, an army invading her brain through the defenseless inner ear. Her head felt swollen, fog-laden. With effort, she opened one eye; the room's brightness stung like a splash of acid. The blurred face of her travel clock read 10:23.

In a panic she jolted upright, but the pounding in her temples sent her slumping back against the mattress. She buried her aching head be-neath the pillow, seeking its downy oblivion, its blessed darkness. If she could only return to sleep, she would forget the sour sea that sloshed in her intestines. She closed her eyes and tried to erase her body. But something nagged her, a notion had grabbed hold of her and she could not shake it loose: *Her daughter, her daughter in the hospital, her daughter needed her.*

The thought of Brenda brought an unexpected wave of queasiness and, with it, the image of a woman with black hair. It was a picture she could not identify, a vision both frightening and confounding; it did not make sense. Emerging from the tent of the pillow, Vera shook her head as if to clear it; she needed to get herself to the hospital before something bad happened.

Without her, who would rub lotion into Brenda's skin so the soap from her sponge bath didn't dry her out? Who else would meticulously check her body for bedsores? Who would be there to remind the doctor that Brenda's breathing had seemed a little rapid just the day before?

Who do you think you're kidding? A voice in her head jeered. *It doesn't make a goddamned bit of difference if you're there or not.* The utterance stunned her, sucked the breath from her lungs. Vera knew this voice, all right, remembered it distinctly, but it had been years since it had come like this. *You might just as well get on a plane and go back to Detroit,* it mocked, *for all the good you're doing. For all Bryn would care.*

A pool of blackness opened just beneath her solar plexus, spreading like oil; Vera knew from experience that if she let it yawn too wide she would be swallowed. Gritting her teeth, she threw back the covers to rise. The gesture sent a cascade of books and miniature bottles crashing to the floor. Four books. Six bottles, their contents drained.

Shakily she stood, and the room spun. For a moment she stared at the scattered objects as if she could not fathom where they might have come from. Then, stepping over the pile, she escaped into the bathroom. Vera shut the door, as if to guard her privacy.

Leaning over the sink, she fought the urge to spew vomit across its pink porcelain. Above the sink's smooth contours, the face in the mirror loomed too large, ghoulish. Vera pressed a warm washcloth to her face, savoring its heat; then she dunked it under cold water to apply to her puffy lids. A dot of toothpaste barely camouflaged the dry and bitter thickness of her tongue.

She spent minimal time on her makeup—a sweep of powder, a swipe of blush, some lipstick—gazing into the mirror without looking herself in the eyes. With comb and hairspray, she tried her best to reconstruct her ruined hairdo, but her fingers felt dull and clumsy. Her temples throbbed.

Emerging from the bathroom, Vera dressed. As much as she tried to hurry, the body would not obey her commands. Putting one foot into the leg of navy blue slacks, she nearly lost her balance and her arm flailed, reaching for the sleeve of a red jacket. Her hand scrabbled on top of the dresser for her earrings—the gold-tone, clip-on pair she'd picked up in the hospital gift shop the day after meeting Djuna's mother—but could find only one.

Just as Vera was set to leave the room, tucking her key card into a pocket of her purse, her eyes once more fell upon the mess on the carpet. She would hate for anyone to get the wrong idea. Without looking at them, Vera shoved the books into one of the bureau drawers and dumped the bottles into a plastic-lined wastebasket. Then she unwound the protective wrapping from the unused water glass and arranged it with its mate on opposite sides of the small table, as if to suggest she'd had a visitor in for drinks.

Outside the air was much too warm for February; it seemed viscous, a difficult medium in which to move. At this late hour of the morning, with midday soon approaching, the customary journey to the hospital took on an unfamiliar air, surreal and sinister. Usually she made the short trek before 6:00 A.M., when the sky was still gray as a pearl, shrouded in the remnants of fog, and the traffic occasional, unhurried. The experience of traveling these streets at that fragile hour was like a dream, private and enclosed, as if the morning itself drew a bubble of protectiveness around her, the sharp edges of the city worn away.

Now, however, that dreamlike sense, the aura of safety, was snatched away by noise and speed and light. Cars gunned their motors and swerved from lane to lane, fierce and ruthless, bent on illicit destinations. The sun reflected every surface hard and slick against her retinas, which felt porous and raw in the noonday glare.

Perspiration soaked her forehead as she trudged past the monolith of the Beverly Center. Last week at dinner Lowell had suggested that Vera walk over to this mall, across the street from the hospital, and have her hair done. "It would be a nice break for you," Lowell had soothed. "Do something for yourself." Vera, who'd been going to the same stylist since Brenda was a teenager, had demurred. The mall looked to her like an armed fortress, and she feared the stylists there would inflict on her a "California look," loose and uncontrolled, instead of teased upward and sprayed into place.

As she entered at last the doors to the hospital, her eyes did not easily adjust to the dimmer, artificial light; bright blotches of color continued to swim in her vision, half blinding her. Her stomach lurched as the elevator climbed, floor by floor, shuddering to every stop.

When she reached Brenda's room, the first person she saw was Djuna. Fury stabbed her; how dare Djuna take advantage of Vera's being sick to encroach upon this time with her daughter? But as her gaze focused, she saw too, seated at the foot of Brenda's bed, a small, middle-aged Chinese woman. Each of the woman's hands was cupped around the soles of her daughter's bare feet with an intimacy that outraged Vera.

"What's going on here?" she demanded, her customary politeness vanishing. "Who the hell are you?"

"Suyuan, this is Vera, Bryn's mother," Djuna hastily crossed the room to stand between them like a referee. "Vera, this is Suyuan, Bryn's acupuncturist."

The Chinese woman turned to greet Vera with a curt nod, her face unsmiling, then abruptly returned her attention to Bryn. The woman did not look like any kind of doctor Vera had ever seen; she wore a flowered-print blouse over loose cotton pants in a violet hue. Long hair, straight and black save for streaks of silver sprouting at her temples, hung unbound to her waist. Vera especially did not trust the intensity of expression on the woman's face as she cradled Bryn's feet in her palms.

"You think you can just bring this woman in here behind my back?" Vera turned on Djuna, her tone shrill with accusation. "You send her away. Dr. Hastings doesn't need any help from *her*." She narrowed her eyes, menacing, "Does he even *know* what you're doing to his patient?"

The Chinese woman regarded her through thick-lensed glasses; their squat black frames sat heavy on her small face. "She is *my* patient," came the unassailable reply. Even through the woman's clipped accent, Vera could hear contempt.

Djuna attempted to intervene. "Bryn's been seeing Suyuan for about eight years. She helped Bryn get sober."

Vera heard the words as if from a great distance, in a tunnel or underwater. Her whole body was trembling; the floor swayed beneath her feet. Why did everything seem to be turning suddenly bizarre, out of her control? Couldn't everyone see she was sick today?

Behind the lenses, the Chinese woman's eyes were magnified, unblinking. "Your daughter's accident caused big shock to the kidney." Her tone contained no deference, no effort of persuasion. "The soul has abandoned the body. She is very deficient; she has no *qi*, no life force. I try to awaken the *shen*, the spirit. Then she can wake up."

Without warning, Vera began to laugh, a sour, mirthless cackle that sprang from the hollow of her throat, from the pool of darkness in her chest that had not drained but just been covered over. Words escaped through the rasps and snorts, syllables strafed the air, propelled by a voice not entirely her own and yet not unfamiliar.

"She's not going to wake up," the voice insisted. "She'll never, *never* wake up," The spasms of laughter turned harsher then, more frantic, bullets spit from the mouth of a Gatling gun.

Djuna had come over to her, was putting her hands on Vera's shoulders, trying to push her into a chair, trying to calm her. Vera could not be sure if the expression on Djuna's face was one of concern or mortification. She knew only that she could not stay in this room.

Struggling against Djuna's grip, she abruptly broke free. She sped from the room, back along the hallway, dodging an old man with a walker, nearly colliding with a young girl in a wheelchair, oblivious to the anxious greetings of familiar nurses. Vera swept past them all and caught the elevator just as the doors were closing. Her heart hammered throughout the slow descent—it had been years since she had run— until at last she reached ground level and burst through the hospital doors into the noontime light.

26.

Bryn

The hand is a boat.
The hull, a cradle
where I rock and sway,
palm curved snug.
I am held.
I am borne.
I am a fish
flown out of the sea
to rest on the shallow deck,
a miracle
in the bright air.

The skin of the hand
is weathered as wood,
grain warmed by sun,
reeking of salt.
A hot sea churns
beneath my belly,
it calls me
but I will not jump.
I cling to the beam,
fingers curl around me
like ribs,
and overhead
looms a swatch of sky
blue and cold,
a merciless eye.

27.

Vera

The mall proved to be as impenetrable as it looked. Breathless and cursing, Vera circled its vast perimeter, seeking a way in. Every door seemed to lead somewhere she did not want to go. She dodged a cluster of teenagers lingering at the guarded entrance to the Hard Rock Cafe, spun past the neon signature of José Eber and the gleaming tiles of the California Pizza Kitchen. She poked her head into each dark maw where cars drove in and exited, and dirt-caked men shook plastic cups at passing vehicles, but she could not find a place for pedestrians to enter.

Her second time around the building, which spanned two city blocks, Vera was forced to confront the two glass-covered escalators that climbed the outside walls like giant centipedes. She nearly gave up then, her stomach still unsettled; she did not relish the prospect of a slow, lurching ascent. The whole idea of window shopping at the mall no longer seemed inviting, but if she did not do this, then what? She could not go back to the hospital now; neither could she bring herself to return to the hotel, her room with its fussy decor, its air of rebuke.

Standing on the sidewalk, baked in the unnatural heat of the February sun, Vera could not imagine any place to go, not in this indifferent city, not anywhere. The traffic whizzed along Beverly Boulevard; tears stung the edge of her eyelids.

Grim-faced, Vera stepped onto the escalator. Gripping the railing, she pressed her eyes shut, willing her stomach to calm as she rose, floor by floor. The last set of ascending stairs deposited her at the rim of the mall, its interior as sterile and forbidding as its façade. It was nothing like the cheerful shopping plazas of the Midwest; there was no wood, no brick, no greenery, nothing to disguise the purpose of the place: commerce, cold and stark.

One of Brenda's nurses—the young one whose brown hair was

cropped much too short—had advised Vera that this was the "coolest" of all the malls. It surprised her that anyone would say that about this place, it was so severe, but then she was reminded of the music videos she'd seen on TV at the hotel, how depressing they appeared, brutal, and, of course, the kids loved them. Unbidden, the image of a black-haired woman returned, her torso in leather, her arms and legs tied down. What was the matter with her? What was that awful picture? Had she seen it on TV? And why did it keep floating before her eyes, drifting up like a toxic bubble to explode and form again?

Bile rose in her throat; perspiration dotted her hairline. Vera leaned against a wall, its marble surface cool on her palms, her forehead. She forced herself to breathe, drawing chilled air into her lungs; she counted slowly to twenty-eight, until her body seemed once more in her control.

Squaring her shoulders, Vera turned to survey the wide corridor of shops, trying to orient herself, to formulate a plan. She was swept by a wave of longing; if only Brenda could be here. They'd always shopped together, from the time her daughter was a little girl, right up until she'd left home; it had been their ritual, soothing and predictable. Chet never cared what they spent as long as Vera was bringing in money from her secretarial jobs; she used to remind Brenda how lucky they were. "A lot of men wouldn't be that way," she'd admonish her daughter, who never seemed to recognize the good qualities in her stepfather.

Brenda always selected beautiful clothes for Vera to try on. "That looks great on you, Mom," she would say, with open admiration, "It's very sexy. Who cares what it costs? You deserve it!" So different from Everett, who would always mumble, "Look at how much they want for that! You don't really need it, do you?" Vera had not done much shopping in the last several years. Everett always made her feel ashamed of her desires, but Brenda encouraged them. The way Chet did.

Before her beckoned the glittering displays of a department store. Vera stepped through the wide archway and was delivered into the cosmetics department. Her nostrils burned from the chemical scent of a dozen perfumes.

She was immediately approached by a petite Frenchwoman in a smart suit, her auburn hair in an attractive coil, her face an exquisite mask. "Madame, would you like to receive a free makeover today?"

Startled, Vera hunched her shoulders, and half turned away. "N-no, no thank you."

"I want you to try our new revitalizer for the skin, it will take years off, and I've got a lipstick color that would look magnificent with your hair and eyes." The woman smiled at Vera as if she could not possibly refuse this offer.

"I'm sorry, I . . . uh . . . I just don't have time today," Vera protested, hoping her trembling voice would signal urgency rather than desperation. She was trying to edge away from the gleaming counters, the vivid displays of compacts and tubes, seductive squares of color, and the soft cloud of the Frenchwoman's perfume that encircled Vera like tentacles.

"That's not a problem," the Frenchwoman assured her in a breathy accent. "I'm going to be here for the rest of the week. Come back tomorrow." Her vermilion lips spread into a smile as she pressed a small card into Vera's palm.

"Uh . . . fine, thank you," Vera murmured as she made her escape. Once she'd fled the cosmetics department, Vera shoved the card into a pocket of her purse.

In the shoe department, no one bothered her. Two bored employees leaned against the cash register exchanging desultory gossip, leaving Vera free to wander unmolested among the tables and pedestals adorned with the latest styles. None of them looked like anything she would wear; she was almost sure she caught a sneer on the face of one of the salesmen as he casually glanced at her cheap, low-heeled shoes. On a whim, Vera plucked up a platform pump, but gasped when she read its price. Were there really women who spent $375 on a pair of shoes?

She abruptly left this department and drifted, aimless, into the juniors department. A grid of video screens occupied one wall, projecting nine identical versions of a black-haired woman who wielded a whip as she growled into a microphone. Vera had been staring at the image for several minutes before noticing that her cheeks were wet, tears dripping from her chin onto the front of her red jacket. With the back of her hand she dabbed at them; she didn't want anyone to see her crying in the middle of the department store, didn't want anyone coming up to ask, "Are you all right?"

Summoning what she hoped was a hurried dignity, Vera approached the young saleswoman behind the register. "Excuse me," she began as the young woman fixed her with a vacant stare. "I've gotten something in my eye," Vera explained, "Can you tell me, where's the ladies room?"

"Shoe department, all the way back," the saleswoman gestured limply in that direction.

"Thank you," Vera offered, but the young woman had already turned her back.

Once she found the restroom, Vera locked herself in a stall. Luckily, the other stalls were vacant; she had the space all to herself. By the time she lowered her body onto the toilet seat, she was sobbing; her choked spasms echoed off the tile. *Stop it,* she commanded herself, *What's wrong with you, carrying on this way,* but she could not stop shaking.

Her insides felt swollen like a blister, tight and putrid, contained by the thinnest membrane. At any moment it would burst, spread poison into every crevice of her system. She tried to swallow, but a fist was stuck in her throat.

Vera sat for a long time, her navy blue slacks bunched around her knees, hugging herself like a child, until she heard the swoosh of an opening door, footsteps leading to another stall, the tinkle of urine against porcelain. Vera blew her nose into a Kleenex, stood, and gathered herself. Once she heard the interloper leave the bathroom, she emerged from the stall. At the sink she washed her hands, then scooped a handful of water from the tap to rinse the brine from her mouth.

Catching her reflection, Vera understood the Frenchwoman's wish to improve her appearance. The skin was blotched and pale, the eyes puffy, the pupils without luster. Her mouth twisted in a scowl. She could barely recognize the woman in the mirror, an old woman, haggard and lost. This was not the way she remembered herself.

Without warning, she pitched forward over the bowl and retched into the sink. She'd eaten nothing since lunch the day before, so what came out of her was just sour liquid, threaded with strings of saliva, a trace of foam.

Vera ran the water once again, quickly, trying to dispose of the mess before anyone could see what she'd done. The image in the glass looked more wretched than before, paler, but the fist in her throat had eased. Vera rooted in her purse, unearthed a stick of gum, Wrigley's, which she folded into her mouth before she left the bathroom.

Directly across from the restroom was a pay phone hanging on the wall. It had escaped Vera's attention the first time she'd passed it, but now, without planning to, she found herself stepping toward it, grasping the receiver, the dial tone soothing in her ear. She located her coin purse, lining up neat piles of quarters, dimes, and nickels on the shelf before her. She deposited two dimes, then her index finger depressed a series of numbers. She was shocked to find that she knew just which keys to push, the number as clear in her mind as if she dialed it every day when, in fact, she had never dialed it.

A mechanical voice instructed her to deposit sixty-five cents for the first three minutes. Vera pressed four quarters into the slot, listened as each *chunked* into the machine. From far away she could hear a phone ringing, and she almost replaced the receiver, but then there was a click as the phone was answered, and Chet's voice said, "Hello."

She almost forgot that she was supposed to answer, caught up instead with the sound of his voice, the graveled brusqueness, soft remnants of his Texas boyhood. She closed her eyes and it was as if he were right next to her, his blue eyes with their taunting, boyish gleam.

"Hello," he said again, impatience bordering on belligerence, and oh, she knew that tone, and this time she answered, "Chet?"

"Vera? Is that you?"

At the sound of her own name her heart speeded up. "Yeah," she said, lapsing into the drawl she only used with him, "It's me."

"Goddamn, girl!" The voice warmed like whiskey in the throat. "This is one hell of a surprise!" Then, more warily, "Is ever'thing all right?"

He doesn't know. The thought was like jolt along her spine. He had no idea, how could he, that she was at this moment standing at a pay phone in a department store somewhere in the middle of Los Angeles. He probably imagined her at home, in the kitchen of the townhouse where she lived with Everett. *But how could he imagine that?* she scoffed. *He's never seen where you live now.*

Chet's voice interrupted this train of thought. "Vera, I asked, are you okay?" Just a hint of menace this time, what he did when a situation looked like it might be beyond his control.

"Yes, sure, I'm fine," she reassured him. Now he expected her to tell him why she'd called, and what was she supposed to say? "I was just . . . uh . . . wondering . . . how . . . how you're doin'."

Chet was great, never been better, he insisted. He loved retirement, not having to be anywhere in particular unless he felt like it, not having to put up with all the bullshit from the SOBs in the front office; now he had time to really live.

Chet loved to talk, Vera remembered, and especially he loved to talk about himself. She wondered, but did not ask, just what "really living" might mean to him at this point in his life. Instead, she let him launch into a story about another ex-wife—Kimberly, his second, Vera being his third—with whom he'd recently had lunch.

"It sure was funny, to see her after all that time," he mused. "It's gotta be—what?—thirty-five years? Y'know, I sat there, and I looked at her, and I didn't feel one fuckin' thing about her. Not love, not hate, just nothin'. It was strange."

It was at this point that the operator broke in, announcing the need for more coins. As Vera slipped in four more quarters, Chet growled, "Where the hell are you, Vera?" wary again, as if she were trying to put one over on him. Suspicion always made him mad.

"I'm at the mall," she answered, so she would not have to feel that she was lying. He'd always been a suspicious man, she recalled, in the way people who lie themselves are often mistrustful. But since Chet also had a strong desire to avoid other people's trouble, he was usually pretty easy to reassure. "I was just thinkin' about you and took a notion to call."

"You didn't want yer husband to know you called me?" he deduced. There was a curl of satisfaction in his tone, as if he were delighted by the hint of intrigue.

"No, Chet," she protested, "it's nothing like that. I just took a notion, that's all."

She was grateful that he didn't press the issue. Instead he continued, "I don't know if I told you, I quit drinkin'. Just gave it up. I haven't had a drink in . . . hell, three, four months. I feel great; I got tired'a bein' so hungover in the morning."

Vera slid the earpiece just away from her ear, pressing the plastic receiver into her temple, where her headache had resumed its pounding. How many times had she heard this in the years since their divorce?

"Oh, yeah," she said, "That's great, Chet. Me, too."

"Really? You don't drink anymore either?" He sounded amazed, although she had told him this on several occasions. "That's goddamn great, isn't it? Y'know, I always used to say we never would'a got divorced if it wasn't for the booze. It was just the 'Days of Wine and Roses' for us, wasn't it, baby?"

Vera closed her eyes and saw herself, years earlier, pacing the living room, waiting for her husband to come home as dawn oozed through the window. She saw the coffee table smashing through the plate glass window. She saw a man in a rage, throwing her down the basement stairs. She saw a bullet spit through the air, bury itself in the wood of the kitchen cabinet. *Oh Chet,* she wanted to say, but didn't, *it was a whole lot more than that.*

"Still, it was fun, though, wasn't it?" He said this like a child who needed to believe in something. "We sure had us some fun times while it lasted."

"Yeah, Chet, I guess we did." She tried to keep the sadness from her voice; her tears had started again, splashing onto the little shelf of the phone booth while she fumbled for a tissue. "Listen, Chet, there's . . . uh . . . another lady here who's been waitin' for a while to use this phone. I think I should be goin'."

"Aw, just tell her to fuck herself," Chet advised, and Vera laughed, a forced, obligatory laugh.

"You take care of yourself, Chet." The pain of the words against her tongue was sharp and brittle, with as many facets as a smashed Christmas ornament.

"All right, Vera, you too. Hey, Vera, you remember what I said about Kimberly?" His voice turned velvet. "That ain't the way I feel about you. I never stopped lovin' you, Vera. I just want you to know that."

His words were string, they tugged at her, insistent; he wanted to hear the same words back from her. It was the least she could do. It wasn't his fault she loved her memory of a man who lived inside her head; maybe Chet had been that man once, or maybe he never was.

She opened her mouth to say what he was waiting for, but her throat closed; it jammed the words inside. All she could manage in reply was, "Thanks."

Vera replaced the receiver in its cradle, scooped up the stacks of coins to return them to her change purse. A perverse guilt began to crawl along her spine, as if she had done something mean by calling—not to herself, but to him. Hurt had soured his voice as he said good-bye.

Hurt sometimes made Chet persistent. He might try to call her, to-morrow or the next day, before he fell off the wagon or after, and Everett, guileless, would say she was in California, might even tell him what had happened to Brenda.

It was only then that Vera realized she hadn't said a word about her daughter, hadn't told Chet anything about the accident, how Brenda hovered, dreamless now, between life and death. It occurred to Vera that she never mentioned Brenda in her conversations with Chet, hadn't done so, in fact, since their divorce. And, although the girl had lived with him for the fifteen years of their marriage, Chet never asked a thing about his stepdaughter.

28.

Djuna

Friday, February 19

For the fifth day in a row, Djuna awoke early and went directly to the hospital, shunning her studio and its urgent telephone, the baleful eye of her camera. In the previous weeks her hospital visits had been a dreadful duty, something—like changing her motor oil or cleaning the cat box—to be put off as long as possible, but now that Bryn was finally showing some improvement, Djuna was eager to get there. Each morning she cursed the other vehicles as she edged her car along the rush-hour freeway, nursing a Styrofoam cupful of bitter coffee from the neighborhood bakery.

This was also the fifth day in a row that Djuna found Vera missing from her daughter's bedside. Each day, Djuna had questioned the staff on the ward, but none of them had seen Mrs. Collins since Monday, when she, in the words of one nurse's aide, ". . . tore outta that room like somethin' was after her." Djuna had also called the hotel several times, but the line to Vera's room was always busy. The messages she'd left went unreturned.

Djuna wanted to pretend that this absence had no particular significance; each day she'd tried to convince herself that *Vera must be busy; she just couldn't make it today.* She didn't want to have to worry about Bryn's mother, but since, as far as she knew, Vera had nothing else here to keep her busy, no other reason to be in Los Angeles, Djuna couldn't help but be concerned about this abrupt change in Vera's routine.

"What the hell got into *her?*" she'd asked Suyuan on Monday, after Vera had dashed from the room. She'd intended it rhetorically, not expecting an answer, but the Chinese doctor had matter-of-factly replied, "That lady is very hungover."

This assessment perplexed Djuna; she would have sworn Bryn had told her that Vera didn't drink anymore. Alcohol was not a part of Djuna's upbringing, and the mysterious power it held over some

145

people—even, at some time before she'd known her, over Bryn—confused her. At any rate, she didn't think she could cope with one more crisis.

I'll give Vera till the end of today, Djuna promised herself, *and if she hasn't shown up by then I'll . . .* In truth, Djuna didn't have a clue what she would do, but she was certain that Bryn would expect her to do something.

Vera didn't even know that Bryn was getting better. Djuna supposed she could have left that message at the hotel desk, but, without knowing what was going on with Vera, she'd decided against it. And "better," of course, was a relative term; Bryn was still in a coma.

The doctors and nurses at the hospital tended to discount the notion that acupuncture was responsible for the changes in Bryn's condition. *No one,* they kept insisting, *knows for sure what factors contribute to a patient regaining consciousness, other than keeping the physical condition stabilized. She might have made these improvements this week anyway,* Djuna had heard several of them say, but even the doctors concurred that the coma seemed to be lessening, and for that, Djuna credited Suyuan.

On Monday, the day of her first visit, the acupuncturist had performed a procedure she called "*qi gong,*" although to Djuna it looked to be no more than a laying on of hands. Suyuan had simply held the soles of Bryn's feet for a very long time; then she had done the same with her patient's upturned palms.

Djuna had been impatient, skeptical. "Aren't you going to put needles into her?" she'd demanded. She knew almost nothing about Chinese medicine. Bryn swore by it, but it made Djuna's skin crawl to think of someone poking needles into her.

Without even bothering to look up, Suyuan had replied, "When deficiency is too severe, you cannot needle. *Qi* is the life force. If there is no *qi* to raise, you cannot raise *qi.*"

By the end of the first treatment, Djuna's doubts had subsided. Bryn's color had improved, her breathing grown deeper, more relaxed. On Tuesday, she had begun to move her left foot—random, involuntary movements, but the first sign of kinetic activity. Later that day, she'd again made a series of small sounds in response to the rhythms of Tito Puente played on the boom box.

Suyuan had returned Wednesday and was pleased to hear of her patient's progress. After carefully fingering each of Bryn's wrists, she'd announced, "She has pulses! Now we can use acupuncture."

Djuna found it repulsive and mesmerizing to watch the long, slender needles penetrate the skin of Bryn's feet and legs, her hands and arms. Amazingly, the insertions drew no blood. At one point, Bryn had moaned as Suyuan slid a needle into a spot below her ankle; although Djuna reached out protectively, as if to shield her lover from some harsh invasion, Suyuan nearly cackled in delight at Bryn's response. "We've reached her," she exclaimed, "and she's talking back! Bryn always has trouble with this point; it's kidney three."

Several hours after the second treatment, Bryn was exhibiting movement in all four of her limbs. She would be completely still for long periods of time, then all of a sudden an arm would jerk, or a fist contract, or a foot jiggle. Djuna had read enough of Emily's faxes to know that the ability to move on both sides of the body was a good sign; it meant that Bryn had at least some functioning in both hemispheres of the brain.

Before she left on Wednesday, Suyuan had advised that Bryn ought to be taken off the anticonvulsive medication she was being given. "She needs her will in order to wake up. Her will is strong, but right now it's having to fight against the drug."

On Thursday, Djuna had made it a point to intercept Dr. Hastings, the neurologist overseeing Bryn's case, as he made his rounds. He was a tall man with a full head of graying hair, a man who'd been handsome in his youth and seemed so accustomed to getting his way that he felt no obligation to charm. Djuna couldn't recall a time she'd seen him smile. He was exactly the kind of man who most antagonized her, a man just like her father, logical, cold, possessed of a certainty that was easily confused with arrogance. Every time she talked to Dr. Hastings, she ended up yelling, and every time she yelled at him she felt like a child, powerless and foolish.

Her most recent fight with him had been her push to have Suyuan treat Bryn. He'd stonewalled for days. "Acupuncture has no demonstrated use in a case like this," he'd intoned.

"How can you not be willing to try?" Djuna had countered, "It's not like your medicine is doing a goddamn thing for her! She's exactly the same!"

"She's still alive," he'd reminded her sternly.

In the end, he'd agreed, but under strict limitations: Suyuan could come only twice a week and, of course, Djuna would have to assume full liability should any complications result from the treatment. He'd made it clear that he had the power to revoke permission at any time.

Thursday's meeting had begun amiably enough. He'd reviewed Bryn's charts, the results of an EEG that showed significant improvement in brain-wave activity in the four days since Suyuan had started working with Bryn, and had to concede, "She seems to be making progress." Still, he'd added, "This might well have happened anyway. The course of coma is highly unpredictable."

In response to hearing Suyuan's suggestion that medication be withdrawn, Dr. Hastings had been unyielding. "That's not only ridiculous," he'd snapped, "it could be extremely dangerous. The anticonvulsive drug we're administering is necessary to prevent seizures," he explained as if to a wayward child determined to play in traffic, "any occurrence of which could produce further damage to the brain."

Before leaving the ward he'd also admonished, "I don't want you to get your hopes too high. Even if the patient does regain consciousness, it's uncertain how much of her normal functioning she'll be able to regain."

It was this conversation Djuna recounted to Suyuan when the acupuncturist arrived Friday morning for her third visit of the week. The Chinese doctor shrugged off the problem of the medication, saying, "Okay, then, we'll have to work with that."

She also refused to join with Djuna in her condemnation of the neurologist. "It is what he has been taught," she reminded Djuna, "No man can know more than he has learned. It must be frustrating to him, to have no answers. Doctors always feel they are supposed to have answers."

"What about you?" Djuna wanted to know, "Don't you have them?"

"Oh, no," the acupuncturist confessed, "Only the patient has the answers. That is always true. Sometimes if I listen well, the patient tells me the answer."

Djuna grew quiet a moment before she asked, "And what does Bryn tell you? Is she going to recover?" She tried to make it sound like a casual inquiry, simple curiosity, but she could not quite mask the undercurrent of fear.

Suyuan was already at work, propping open Bryn's eyelids to gaze at the pupils, running her fingers along the pulse points at Bryn's wrists. "Oh, yes," she assured Djuna. "She wants to. I wish they'd let me come sooner, because the longer she's away, the more difficult to return. But, yes. I know Bryn; she's very strong, she has the will. If there's damage to her brain she'll create new pathways. A creative person can do that."

Djuna drank in those words, letting them flow into her like a rain of hope. Then the Chinese woman fixed Djuna with a sharp look. "Are you willing to get into trouble?"

Djuna shrugged. "What do you have in mind?"

Suyuan drew closer, as if to disclose a secret. "I want to get Bryn out of bed," she explained, "to get her sitting up. I'll need your help to do it. I'm not even supposed to be here today; if we get caught, they'll throw me out of here for good." Suyuan seemed energized by the element of risk.

"Is that a good idea?" Djuna fretted. "To get her up, I mean?"

"Oh, yes, very good," Suyuan assured her, "It will help the blood to circulate, and remind her to wake up."

Remembering Dr. Hastings and his warnings, Djuna had misgivings, but she forced herself to put them aside. Bryn would not have hesitated; she would do whatever Suyuan recommended. "So how do we do it?"

Suyuan had clearly thought it out. "In the hall, there's a wheelchair; no one is using it right now. You go get it."

"Just . . . uh . . . wheel it in?"

"That's right."

"What if somebody sees me?" Djuna had never been good at subterfuge; Bryn always said that every thought in Djuna's brain could be read across her face.

"Don't let that happen," Suyuan admonished.

Djuna poked her head beyond the door to make sure the hallway was clear. She spied the vacant chair and strolled out the door, in an elaborate display of nonchalance. When she reached the wheelchair, she grasped its handles with authority and pushed, but it would not budge. She tried again, and still the wheels would not move. Djuna dashed back into the room.

"I can't move it," she told Suyuan, "Now what do I do?"

"You have to release the brake," the acupuncturist explained, losing patience.

Djuna went back into the hall. This time Penny, one of the day nurses, was coming down the corridor.

"Morning, Djuna, how's it going?" Was it only Djuna's imagination or did she seem unduly curious?

"Everything's fine, Penny, no problem!" Djuna responded, just a little too heartily.

"That's good. I've got some tests I'll need to run on Bryn this morning; I'll be in there in a little while."

Now Djuna broke into a sweat. As soon as Penny disappeared into another room, Djuna knelt to examine the wheels of the chair. At last she found the lever, released the brake, and delivered the chair to Bryn's room.

"Bring it over here, right beside the bed," Suyuan instructed.

"Do you still think we should do this?" Djuna asked, "Penny said—" but Suyuan interrupted.

"Don't waste time! We need to lift her—she'll be heavy, like dead weight—and take care not to disengage the feeding tube or the catheter." She pointed out the spots where each device connected to Bryn's body. "Once she's in the chair, we need to tie her to it—we can use the sheet. She won't be able to sit up by herself."

Djuna regarded Bryn on the bed; her body looked fragile as a rag doll's. "Are you sure this won't hurt her?" she asked plaintively.

Suyuan did not take time for extra reassurances. Instead, she unleashed the wrist restraints. "Come on," she urged, "you take her feet." Stationed at the head of the bed, Suyuan gently rolled Bryn to an upright position, then nodded the signal for Djuna to grab her legs and lift. Swallowing her apprehension, Djuna obeyed. She was astonished to feel the substance of her lover's body, not fragile at all, but weighty, a presence to be reckoned with. She was astounded too by the strength in Suyuan's small, compact figure. In a single motion, they settled Bryn's body into the chair.

"Hold her in that position," Suyuan ordered as she yanked the sheet from the bed and bound Bryn's torso to the back of the chair. She double-checked the lines of the catheter and feeding tube, making sure there was no obstruction. She arranged her patient's arms so that they rested on the armrests, her feet on the footpads. Bryn's head lolled forward until her chin met her chest.

"How long does she stay that way?" Djuna sent an anxious glance in the direction of the door.

Suyuan was pulling needles out of her briefcase, positioning them at various points on Bryn's limbs. Today she also slid one into the skin above Bryn's heart, and two into the top of her scalp. Once the needles were in place, she again monitored Bryn's pulses.

They heard footsteps approaching and each looked at the other for a long, suspended moment, Djuna scarcely breathing, until Emily clacked through the door in brown suede pumps and a double-breasted suit. "I had a meeting out of the office and thought I'd drop by . . . Holy Mother!" she squealed as her eyes fell on Bryn in the wheelchair.

"Shh, keep it down," Djuna warned. "We're trying not to get busted here. Emily, this is Suyuan—" but Emily already knew the acupuncturist, for years, Emily explained, before Djuna had even met Bryn.

Watching them exchange greetings, Djuna was once more reminded of all the years Bryn had lived without her, a whole life she hadn't shared. It was like an ache inside her, these parts of Bryn she could never know.

"What's going on here?" Emily demanded. Djuna briefly explained.

"Want me to be the decoy?" Emily offered, "If a nurse comes near the room I'll drop to the floor in a dead faint and distract their attention!"

She and Djuna watched in silence as Suyuan twisted the slender needles between her fingertips, rotating them beneath the surface of Bryn's skin. A few minutes passed, and Emily asked, "Have you heard anything from Vera?"

Djuna sighed and shook her head.

"I found out something last night that may shed some light on the subject," Emily's blue eyes grew wide behind her glasses frames; her voice gained speed. "I had a phone conversation with Lowell, just a 'Hi, how are you?' kind of a thing; we probably talk once a quarter, you know? I asked her how her dinner with Vera had gone, because—

remember?—that was the night I was here, and she told me a little bit about it.

"Then she casually mentions, 'Oh, and I brought her back to the house and gave her my copies of all of Bryn's books.' I, of course, flipped out: 'Lowell, are you out of your mind? The last thing Bryn ever wanted was for her family to get their hands on her work!' But Lowell acted like she just couldn't understand what I was getting all worked up about."

Emily removed her glasses for dramatic effect before posing the question, "Do you think Vera read them and wigged out?"

Djuna raked a hand through the fringe of her spiky hair. "Fuck!" she groaned. "What am I supposed to do about that?"

In her chair, Bryn started to thrash and moan. Suyuan hurried to pluck the needles from her flesh. "Hold her," she ordered Djuna, "Don't let her fall."

Terrified, Djuna gripped Bryn's shoulders in a bear hug. Much as she tried to silence it, her last conversation with Dr. Hastings kept replaying in her mind, the precautions necessary to prevent further injury to the brain. What were they doing here?

Bryn's neck was no longer limp; her head was upright, her face turning from side to side, its features contorted by something that looked like rage or pain. Her arms reached out, fingers clawing at the air, her feet kicked against the footrests, blind, incoherent gestures.

Djuna struggled to contain her; Emily rushed to help, but there seemed to be a force within Bryn that could not be quieted. Finally, Djuna cupped her hand at the back of Bryn's scalp, spreading her fingers, caressing the surface of the skin. It was a sensation that had always delighted Bryn, who said it reminded her of being an infant and having her head held, her whole brain in the palm of someone's hand.

This seemed to soothe her. Her movements grew calmer, less frantic, the tension appeared to leave her body, her breathing quieted. Her face eased into blankness, hands fluttering just a little before they sank into her lap.

Her head, though, remained upright, and when Djuna leaned close to whisper in her ear, "It's okay, baby, it's gonna be all right, little pie," Bryn seemed to turn in her direction, as if listening.

29.

Djuna

Friday, February 19

As she stepped through the double glass doors, flanked on both sides by trees adorned with a profusion of twinkling white lights, it struck Djuna that she had not been back to the hotel since she'd checked Vera in over two weeks ago. At that time, she'd thought the place charming and had congratulated herself on finding such an expedient solution to the problem of what to do with Vera: *a small hotel, close to the hospital, and very pleasant, too.* Now the decor struck her as cloying, everything forced and artificial. It was the kind of environment her own mother would love, she realized, but probably not Vera.

She recalled how Vera had protested, sputtering demurrals as Djuna had carried her suitcase to the room, but at the time Djuna had refused to recognize these as genuine pleas against exile. Now, walking the carpeted halls under glittering chandeliers, past vases sprouting elaborate floral statements, Djuna could taste Vera's loneliness in the scented air.

Guilt hummed through the ornate corridor, hissed at Djuna from each doorway she passed. She'd treated Vera as an intruder, something to be disposed of as efficiently as possible. It was one thing for Bryn to have issues with her mother, broken links in the bond between them, but she would still expect Djuna to treat Vera with kindness, as Bryn had done unfailingly with Rose.

Djuna paused outside the door to Vera's room, uncertain what would greet her on the other side. A Do Not Disturb sign dangled from the door handle. Wiping her damp palms on the leg of her jeans, she cleared her throat and knocked.

Her approach was met with silence, so Djuna tapped again, more insistent this time. Then, placing her mouth close to the door, she called, "Vera, it's me, Djuna. Are you asleep?"

"Go away!" came Vera's muffled voice from behind the door.

"Please, Vera, I need to talk to you!"

"I don't want to talk. Go away." Vera sounded as if her mouth were stuffed with cotton.

"Vera, listen," Djuna gripped the handle of the door as if her words could make it turn. "It's about Bryn. She's getting better! Today she started to open her eyes!"

There was a long moment, then she heard footsteps. The handle twisted beneath her fingers, and the door swung open.

The room was a wreck, wrinkled sheets in a tangle on the bed, clothing strewn across chairs and on the floor, the tabletop and dresser littered with glasses and small bottles. Vera's face was drawn; sharp hollows ringed her eyes. Her lipstick was a smear across her face, her hair a ruin. Her clothes, the same ones Djuna had seen her wear on Monday, were creased and disheveled. A sour smell rose from her body.

This was shocking to Djuna; it was impossible to reconcile Vera's customary tidiness with the ravaged woman before her. Even when she had the flu, her own mother was always attired as if company were just about to arrive; Djuna wondered how many times in her life Bryn had found Vera in this condition. The sight embarrassed Djuna, as if she'd intruded on a moment she was not supposed to witness.

Vera had collapsed into one of the chairs, on top of a discarded bathrobe. She huddled there, shoulders hunched, hands between her knees, like a child prepared to receive a scolding.

"Vera," Djuna began, "I've been so worried about you."

"I'm sorry," Vera kept her eyes on the floor.

"I don't mean it like that!" Djuna bit her lip. She was going to have to rein in her impatience for this to go well. "I mean," she walked over to Vera and crouched in front of her, "I know you've been having a hard time, and I'm . . . concerned about you."

A half hope rose like a crescent moon in Vera's eyes as she faced Djuna for the first time. It reminded Djuna of the eyes of a stray cat, abandoned, abused, wanting to trust, but fearful.

"Tell me about Brenda," Vera sighed.

Djuna described the progress of the last few days. ". . . and just before I left today," Djuna continued, "she opened her eyes for the first time. Just a few times, like blinking. The nurses told me she can't *see* anything yet, sort of like a baby when it first gets born and hasn't learned how to focus, but this means she's starting to wake up!

"I thought you might want to go over there with me and see her tonight."

At this suggestion, Vera's face slammed shut, the moon eclipsed, her mouth set in a hard line. "I don't think I want to do that right now," she mumbled.

"Vera," Djuna placed a tentative hand on Vera's shoulder, "I heard about . . . how Lowell gave you Bryn's books." She hesitated, then, barely raising her voice above a whisper, asked, "Did you read them?"

Vera made a sharp inhalation of breath, sucked quickly through clenched teeth, then held in. Her face seemed to cave in on itself, the features drawn sharper, hollows deepening. Slowly, her eyes filled, tears pooling at the rims but not spilling over.

In a flat, strangled voice, she said, "She hates me, doesn't she?"

Djuna felt the swell of Vera's sorrow; it eddied around her, a dangerous turbulence. Djuna searched the room for a life raft; her eyes found the television. An image was projected but the sound was mute. On screen, four skinny men performed a strutting dance; sometimes they plucked at guitars, at other times they seemed to menace a pouty young woman in a schoolgirl's uniform. Djuna thought it incredible that Bryn's mother was watching MTV, yet another thing her own mother would never do.

She forced herself to return her gaze to Vera, reached out and took one of her hands. The hand was jittery, a captured bird; at any second it might fly away. "Vera, Bryn doesn't hate you, she just . . ."

But really, Djuna didn't know what to say. She thought of Rose, the ragged knot of love and pity and contempt that irretrievably connected them; how could it ever be explained?

Instead, Djuna continued, "Bryn has always told me that no matter what she writes, it's only part of what is in her heart."

She couldn't tell if Vera had heard her words, or found in them any shred of reassurance. Vera seemed to be staring at the painting that hung above the bed, a flock of parrots rendered in an irritating palette of tropical pigments, overstated oranges, greens, and blues. Still, the hand Djuna held seemed to soften a little, the palm fitting more comfortably against her own.

"When Brenda was a little girl," Vera began in a voice so tremulous it sounded like it came from underwater, "I used to come into her room at night, and I'd look down at her and . . . I wouldn't recognize her. Had her eyes always been that shape? Didn't her mouth used to be more round? It was like her face had changed when I wasn't looking. I wondered if someone had come in the night and exchanged their little girl for mine. . . ."

She began to cry in earnest now, a full-throated keening that Djuna had once in a while seen in Bryn, after their worst fights, the ones that left them hopeless, certain they would never find a way back to each other. Djuna held Vera in an awkward hug, patting her arm and rocking just a little, until Vera calmed down. Then Djuna retrieved the Kleenex box from where it lay under the bed.

She knew what she had to do. "Vera," she said abruptly, "I've been a *putz*, and I'm really sorry about it. What do you say we get you out of this hellhole?"

Vera turned toward her, eyes red-rimmed and uncomprehending.

"Let's pack up your bags and check you out of here," Djuna urged. "It won't take much work to make the spare room livable. And on our way home, we'll stop and have some dinner." Once the words were spoken, it seemed easy, inevitable, like plunging into the ocean when she was a kid, the fear all in the anticipation. Now there was only surrender, lifting her feet from the sand, then falling into the embrace of water.

Vera had withdrawn her hand from Djuna's grasp. She seemed edgy, uncertain, and Djuna wondered whether she'd miscalculated, if Vera would prefer to stay here after all. The older woman scanned the room, eyes lingering on the painting, the television screen, the wrecked bed.

"If it's all right," she said finally, "I think I'd like to take a shower before I go."

"No problem," Djuna assured her. "Why don't I go downstairs and settle up the bill while you get ready. Take all the time you need."

"I feel like I should make a contribution—" Vera began, but Djuna stopped her.

"I told you from the beginning I'd take care of it, and I will."

Vera nodded carefully. "Thank you. And . . . maybe I could go in the morning to see Brenda?"

"I'll drive you over first thing."

Retracing her path down the carpeted hallway, Djuna felt light, al-

most optimistic, for the first time since the accident. Even standing before the cashier, writing a check that would drain most of the balance
she and Bryn had saved for a summer trip to Paris, Djuna signed the
draft with a satisfied flourish. Things were changing now; they would
be okay. The long siege was over.

30.

Bryn

The wet green planet spins,
or is it me,
strapped to this Catherine wheel,
whirling,
bones turned to jelly,
teeth rattled like dice,
everything unshaped?
Velocity flattens into
smears of color,
streaks of shadow,
light;
a violent centrifuge,
it separates my elements—
blood,
breath,
language,
ghosts—
then hurls me
into chaos
where I spin.
I am the axis,
twirling hands
on a clock's blank face,
time pushed
to the brink,
dizzying words scrawled
on a prayer wheel.

Then the turning slows,
but I don't notice,
still caught

in a blur of speed,
the bright slap
of wind.
My hair no longer
streams behind me,
taut as if pulled
by strings;
the whine of the axle
subsides.
My bones are suspended
in oil,
float unseen
in a viscous ocean.
Time stops,
the glass cracks
then melts.
Around me,
shadows loom,
their thick tongues
clumsy with speech.

31.

Vera

Vera stood at the kitchen sink, hot water streaming over her hands as she rinsed her supper dishes. There weren't many—she'd done no more than heat a can of soup and toast some bread—but she took her time with them, comforted by the warm spray of water.

Stacking the dishes in the drainer, she left them to air-dry, as was the custom of this household. When she'd first come here a week ago she'd had to fight the urge to rearrange the cupboards and scour the countertops—her daughter and Djuna were indifferent housekeepers—but after Djuna's polite but insistent protests, Vera had suppressed her urge to clean. She was a guest here, she reminded herself; she supposed she could learn to tolerate the grime caked into corners of the linoleum and piles of papers and books that seemed to sprout, like fields of weeds, from every horizontal surface.

Vera sighed and stared out the window above the sink; its night-blackened pane reflected her own face. Djuna had gone tonight to have dinner with those young men, Brenda's students, the ones who'd come to see her. Vera had been invited too, but she'd begged off, worn out from her day at the hospital.

She'd come to dread her daily visits. In the days of Brenda's coma, Vera had been content to sit beside the bed, lulled by the soft beeps of the monitors and the low rasp of her daughter's breathing, by the *stillness* of coma. She'd kept then the vigil of the gardener, content to know the bulbs were tucked beneath the earth, waiting for their season to bloom.

What had blossomed, though, was monstrous, lurid, and carnivorous; her daughter was unrecognizable, more like a wild, demented animal than the purposeful girl Vera remembered. The more consciousness Brenda regained, the more uncontrollable she grew. Without adequate sedation or restraint, Brenda thrashed and clawed, spewing curses at all who came near. She grabbed at her IV, yanked her feeding tube; she moaned and babbled.

Dr. Hastings called it "remarkable progress" that Brenda had so quickly moved to this level of awareness, and Djuna seemed so buoyed by Brenda's animation that she did not mind if Brenda screamed or shrank from her. But Vera could not share their optimism. If her deepest fear had been that her daughter would die, here then was a possibility far worse: that Brenda might live for years in this condition.

Vera sighed again and paced the kitchen, her soft-soled bedroom slippers shuffling on the linoleum. Loneliness veiled her shoulders like the fog enshrouding the streets beyond the window. She realized, with a faint surprise, that she missed Djuna; they had spent so much time together this past week. Just last night, over Chinese dinner, Vera had found herself telling Djuna about her first husband, Carl, how young and dumb she'd been when she married him, how mean he'd turned out to be. Carl was Brenda's actual father, not that it made any difference; neither mother nor daughter had seen hide nor hair of him in almost forty years.

"Yeah, Bryn calls him her 'sperm donor,'" Djuna had interjected, laughing in a way that made Vera feel included, not judged. By the time the fortune cookies were delivered, Djuna was talking about her father and the many affairs he'd had during her parents' marriage.

"It's supposed to be this big secret," she'd sneered. "And all my brothers and sisters pretend not to know about it, but I can't live like that. Several years ago I confronted Sid; I told him I knew and that it made me sick. As a result, we don't see much of each other."

Watching the way Djuna's fist curled against the tabletop, Vera had glimpsed a vulnerability that was ordinarily shielded by the tough exterior. On impulse, she had reached across the table, threading her hand between the tiny teacups to cover the clenched fist, and Djuna had not pulled away.

Then Vera shared her fortune, a curl of paper salvaged from the fragments of stale cookie. "Something you wish for will come true," Djuna read aloud and grinned. "That's great!"

Vera had shrugged. "I guess when you get to be my age, you run out of things to wish for."

Djuna's eyebrows had arched in puzzlement. "What about just wishing for Bryn to be all right?"

Vera had laughed, feigning agreement. She hadn't the heart to say she was afraid to wish for that, afraid to set too high an expectation. Djuna seemed to have no doubt that her love would be restored to her, Snow White awakened by a kiss. Djuna's faith, Vera saw, was not in God or medicine, nor in any kind of optimism that things turn out for the best. Instead, Djuna had placed her faith in Brenda, in the certainty of their bond. It was like trusting that the sun would shine again, unthinkable that it would not.

But, pacing once more to the blackened pane in Djuna's kitchen, Vera could imagine everlasting darkness, oblivious to her prayers or the turning of the earth. What she'd seen so far of her daughter's recovery did not inspire hope. In the week since Brenda's reawakening, her daughter had not recognized any of the people who visited her bedside. Although her eyes were open, and she would follow and track movement in the room, no spark of knowing ever lit her face. She would sometimes respond to hearing her name, whether "Brenda" or the self-chosen "Bryn," but that reaction was just as likely to be a retching sound or the slam of her fist against the mattress.

She resisted every effort to approach her physically, jerked away from the proffered embrace as viciously as she fought the aide who tried to change her sheets. Her coordination was still poor and her blows rarely achieved the target at which they were aimed, but there was no mistaking the strength of their intention.

Only two things seemed to calm her, aside from the drugs that sucked her each night into slumber. One was music played on the stereo beside the bed, especially if nothing else was going on in the room to distract her. It appeared to be the one stimulus on which Brenda was able to focus her attention. Her eyes would narrow in concentration, the rigidity in her body would ease; she seemed to be listening carefully to each note, as if here at last was a language she could understand.

The other calming influence was Suyuan. The acupuncturist was the one person from whom Brenda did not recoil, whose approach was not batted away. Suyuan never talked to Brenda in the cheerful patter of the doctors and nurses: "Hi, Bryn, how's it goin' today?" or "You're lookin' good today, Bryn." She would always come to the side of Brenda's bed and look deeply into her eyes for a long moment, as if their gaze held conversation. Brenda would visibly relax, allowing her mouth to untwist from its angry scowl. She let Suyuan take her hand and hold it, uttering only the softest moans of protest when the needles were slipped into her flesh.

The first few days Vera had had to leave the room during these treatments, to escape the knot that tightened in her throat, a jealousy that Suyuan, not she, had won her daughter's trust. Vera did not think she would ever warm to the woman's forbidding personality, but she had gained an admiration for her manner with Brenda, the way her daughter seemed to surrender her fierce will to Suyuan's ministrations. After Suyuan's visits, Brenda would usually sleep, not the sedated slumber of the hospital night but a genuine repose, complete with REM. Vera wondered what it was her daughter dreamed.

Aside from an impressive vocabulary of profanities, Brenda had little language. The words she did speak seemed unrelated to the situation at hand, and her syntax was impenetrable. "Fly look rain isn't," was her response to a question about whether she was warm enough.

Vera shook her head as if to clear the thoughts that swarmed inside her mind. A chill traveled the width of her shoulders; she left the kitchen, wrapping her bathrobe more tightly around her body, pausing in the hall to raise the thermostat. At home, Everett would never allow it to go above seventy degrees, not even in winter, but Djuna had said, "Turn it as high as you need to be comfortable."

A noise outside made her start. Vera felt herself adrift, alone in this house that was not her own. She supposed she could watch TV, but Djuna had only a small portable, and no cable; "Bryn *hates* TV," Djuna had explained, apologetic. The living room walls were lined with bookshelves, but the sheer volume of possibilities intimidated Vera, who had not been much in the mood for reading lately anyway. A glance at her wristwatch showed it was only 8:30, too early to go to bed.

The second door off the hallway led to the room Brenda used as an office. When Vera had last visited this house, Brenda had kept the door to this room closed; Vera had never seen it. She hesitated now beside the entrance, then turned the knob and let the door swing open. Immediately, Toulouse skittered out of nowhere, seizing the opportunity to slip past her legs and enter the room. The air inside was colder than the rest of the house, and carried a faint aroma she could not identify, spicy and exotic. It reminded Vera of the incense her daughter would burn in her bedroom as a teenager; only later had Vera learned its purpose, to camouflage the smell of marijuana.

In a far corner, a candle flickered in a tall glass, casting a dim glow and ghostlike shadows. Vera did not approve of fire left burning unattended, and she almost crossed the room to extinguish it, then stopped herself. Djuna must have a reason to leave it lit, she told herself. Instead, Vera reached into the room and found the wall socket, flicking on the overhead light.

It was a small room, painted creamy yellow. Brenda had always loved strong colors in her environments; Vera could recall a jewel green bathroom from one long-ago apartment, a bedroom in Lowell's house painted the color of rubies. In this room, the primary decor was clutter. A desk sat before a tall window that faced the garden, the surface crowded with books and file folders, loose papers, notes scrawled on scraps. Jutting out from this desk was another table, supporting a computer, its screen dark. Four upright filing cabinets, legal sized, commanded the full length of a wall. Above them were long wooden shelves, bowed with books.

Wary as a trespasser, Vera stepped in. She had the sense of stealing into a forbidden sanctum; she felt both the danger and thrill of transgression. Although there was no way her daughter could find out she had been here, Vera was nagged by an irrational fear of discovery and retribution.

Against the inside wall was an antique settee with faded green upholstery, torn in places by age and cat claws; Toulouse was curled against a pillow at one end. He stared at her impassively; Vera was struck with the wild notion that he would be the one to tell on her.

Before the sofa sat a low coffee table, piled with magazines and more books. A half drunk cup of tea grew a layer of mold; Vera had to check her impulse to remove it. On the wall above the settee was a large framed photograph of a night sky; against blackness, stars whirled and spun, converging into an image that seemed almost like a human form, though Vera could discern no distinct features.

The fourth wall was covered with framed photos of all sizes, hung in a jumble of styles and eras. There was a picture of Brenda from when she'd been an actress, wearing a medieval-style pointed hat draped with a blue veil, looking young and terribly sincere. Beside this was a snapshot of Djuna, blowing a kiss to the camera. To one side was a picture of Lowell, taken about the time Vera had first met her, and a snapshot of Emily, Brenda's friend who came nearly every day to the hospital.

In a small gilt frame was an image of Brenda at eight, already serious, staring gravely at the lens. That was paired with an aging Polaroid of Djuna at probably the same age, wearing striped pajamas and a gigantic pair of men's shoes. Below these two hung another portrait of Brenda, provocatively posed in a bustier, leaning forward, pouting for the photographer.

Elsewhere on the wall was Vera's high-school graduation photo; Vera wondered what Brenda saw in that girl with the smooth, blank face and faraway eyes. There was a photo-booth strip of Vera and Brenda together, the girl gazing at her mother with such adoration it made Vera's heart hurt to see it. Central in the cluster of photographs was a picture of Vera's mom and dad, taken well before Brenda was born. A handsome man held a comely woman in his lap, her arms around his neck, his head tilted back in passion, and they were laughing.

Vera couldn't apprehend this image of her parents without recalling others: her father shaking her by the shoulders, knocking over chairs, red-faced with rage and screaming; her mother in tears, collecting shards of broken china, pressing an ice bag against raw bruises. Vera had never told her daughter most of that; she'd wanted Brenda to love her grandparents. Now, though, it seemed unjust to have this photo there, as if a rebuke to Vera; there were no pictures of any of *her* husbands.

Toulouse stirred only slightly, stretching one paw in her direction, when she plopped down beside him on the settee. The yellow walls glowed around her as if she were inside a bright lantern. Feeling overcome, she reached up and turned out the incandescent light, plunging the room into murky grayness. Only the tiny candle flame remained, sputtering in the corner, illuminating nothing.

Vera stared at the outlines of the frames against the wall. As if, like Toulouse, she could see in the dark, Vera still saw the images contained in those frames; they blurred and swam together in her vision. Each became an element of a story, one version of the story Brenda told herself about her life.

32.

Djuna

The first hint of light caught the haze in the air, turning the sky the same color as the landscape, a dull dun. At this predawn hour, the highway was deserted. Djuna flicked off her headlights, the strip of road scarcely darker than the space surrounding it, and let her car speed east.

She'd wanted to be in the desert before the sun rose, wanted to be there to watch those first rays glittering at the rim of the horizon. She wanted to be alone in the vast desolation, to feel the earth stretching away from her in every direction. Perhaps here her camera could work its magic once again, could find some presence amidst the emptiness.

Djuna drove, shunning the radio, content with the whistle of air through her partially opened window, the low hum of tires on pavement. Her eyes burned from squinting through the murky light. To her left she saw, spread over the rise of hills, the outline of a hundred windmills, their arms spindly, whirling against the gray sky.

Emily had agreed to drive Vera to the hospital today, and it only made sense, since Djuna had no place there any longer. Djuna took a gulp of thermos coffee, its acid bite a perfect match for her own bitterness. *The most important thing is that Bryn gets well,* she reminded herself. It wasn't as though she'd lost sight of that fact, she'd just never imagined that her lover's recovery might not include her.

Over the past two weeks, and with Suyuan's care, Bryn had made remarkable improvements. She'd regained some muscular control and a rudimentary command of speech. She could answer questions with simple sentences, and more often than not they were appropriate to what had been asked. In the last few days she had even begun to make analogies, as when she'd requested a bath, complaining that her body smelled like "sour dust." She could now feed herself and was relearning in occupational therapy how to brush her teeth, comb her hair, and fasten buttons.

It must have been about ten days ago that Bryn had started to recognize people, beginning with Vera. One afternoon she had suddenly looked up into her mother's face, put out her hand and whispered, "Mama?" Vera, eyes streaming, had swooped to embrace her.

Petty as she knew it was, this had made Djuna just a little sad; *she'd* wanted to be the first, to be the most important. But, with Evelyn's help, she'd resolved those feelings; after all, it was crazy to try to compete with that maternal bond, no matter how frayed the knot might be.

A day later, Bryn greeted Suyuan by name. This didn't trouble Djuna, who was convinced that Bryn, even in coma, had some profound connection to Suyuan. The imperturbable acupuncturist had not treated Bryn's salutation as a big event, but merely nodded and instructed, "Show me your tongue, please."

When, a week ago, Bryn had smiled and said hello to Emily, Djuna once more felt a pang of regret. Emily had been an exceptionally devoted friend, and had known Bryn for years longer than Djuna had. Still, before her accident, Bryn often declared that there was no one on the planet she loved as much as Djuna, and Djuna had taken it as a vow.

All the while Djuna kept presenting herself for Bryn's inspection, only to be treated like a stranger, or worse, an intruder. Bryn's eyes would flick over her, searching the room for someone familiar, and when Djuna tried to speak to her, Bryn would either not respond or grow agitated. If Djuna tried to take her hand or brush a lock of hair from her forehead, Bryn would combat the gesture with a feral intensity.

Djuna tried to maintain patience. Dr. Hastings had explained that no one could recover from a head injury as severe as Bryn's all at once, that capabilities would come back piecemeal, bits of memory, portions of vocabulary, random habits. Some might never be restored, with no way to predict or understand why. Suyuan, too, had counseled, "She's working very hard right now. Don't put too much pressure on her. Give her time."

Djuna tried to follow this advice, until last Tuesday night. Djuna had been with Bryn since early afternoon, mostly seated at a slight remove from the bed, occasionally trying to talk to her, with no success.

Just after 6:00, Lowell came into the room, and Djuna had nearly screamed when Bryn's eyes lit with joy and her mouth formed Lowell's name. This was only the second time Lowell had even come to the hospital. All of Djuna's hard-won patience seemed to evaporate.

Unable to restrain herself, Djuna had pressed harder. She tried talking about things they'd done together, described the house they shared, used the pet names they reserved for one another. She'd brought in a snapshot of the two of them, taken last summer at Point Lobos on the Monterey Peninsula. Not only did Bryn not recognize Djuna, she did not seem able to identify herself either. "Who are they?" she'd scowled and flung the picture on the floor.

Vera was distraught about it, and tried to help. She'd say things to her daughter like, "Djuna's been so good to bring me here every day" and "I don't know what I'd do without Djuna," but Bryn remained blank.

Yesterday, Djuna had asked Vera to go down to the coffee shop, to leave them alone for a bit. Perhaps, with no one else in the room, Bryn might be forced to come to terms with her. Seated in a chair beside the bed, Djuna repeated the speech she had carefully rehearsed the night before.

"Bryn, I really need to talk to you. This is Djuna, remember? For the last four years we've been in love with each other. We live together, we have a house in Silverlake—"

She paused because Bryn was shaking her head in violent disagreement. "I don't . . . live . . . not . . . Silverlake," she insisted.

"Then where do you live?" Djuna shot back, too eagerly; these were the first words Bryn had spoken in direct response to her.

Bryn's features clenched in confusion; she appeared to be searching her brain for the answer. Djuna held her breath. Finally Bryn mumbled, "I live . . . here."

Djuna began to cry hard, making a futile effort to wipe tears and snot with the back of her hand, forcing her words between sobs. "Pie, I love you so much. Ever since your accident, I've been crazy with fear. I don't know what I'd do without you. . . ."

The sight of Djuna's tears seemed first to alarm, then anger Bryn. Her face darkened, and she began to shout, "Don't know you . . . can't help . . . get out, go, out!"

Her screams had drawn two nurses and Dr. Hastings, who'd come on the ward for his rounds. The nurses set to work calming Bryn—Djuna noticed one of them preparing an injection—and Dr. Hastings was left to comfort the inconsolable Djuna. He'd hastily swept her from the room, leading her to a sitting area farther down the hall. There he guided her onto a brown sofa.

From his pocket he'd produced a pressed handkerchief, which he offered. It smelled of starch and tobacco. He waited as she wiped her eyes and blew her nose, then took a seat himself in an adjacent chair. From this perch, he leaned forward, as if to diminish the distance between them.

"Djuna, I understand that this is very hard for you—" he'd begun.

"She doesn't even know who I am!" Djuna wailed, and more tears spouted into the doctor's handkerchief.

She would never have pegged him for a man who easily dealt with the expression of emotion, but yesterday afternoon he'd nodded gravely in response to her outburst, then given her time to compose herself. Perhaps he was not as much like Sid as she'd once thought.

"Let me tell you what we know," he said, when her sniffling had once more subsided. "From the reports of the people who've been working closely with Bryn the last few weeks, a pattern seems to be emerging. Bryn has shown a good recall of her childhood and adolescence, even her young adult years. She remembers her mother, she recognizes her old friends. And she seems to have no trouble with the people she's just recently encountered, like the nurses and therapists she's met since she regained consciousness."

He had paused then to look at Djuna, to make sure that she was following his words. "What she does not appear able to remember is anything regarding the last five years of her life. When we ask her age, she seems confused about it. When we ask where she lives or what she does for work, she isn't sure. You've told us she's published four books, but she told the physical therapist she's written two."

"What are you saying?" Djuna demanded. His words had made her furious. "You mean it's just wiped out of her brain? The last five years? She couldn't possibly forget her writing! Our relationship? Like someone pushed the goddamned delete button?"

He'd stood her rage without striking back. "It's more like this," he said gently, "Have you ever lost a file on your PC? You know the information is in there, somewhere, but you can't find the right code to retrieve it?

"Bryn has a form of retroactive amnesia," he'd continued. "It's not uncommon with this kind of injury. At this point, we don't know for certain whether its cause is psychogenic, that is, a response to the emotional trauma of the accident, or whether there is actual neurological impairment."

Remembering this conversation, Djuna heard again the droning that had filled her head in that hospital sitting room, the low-pitched burr that had nearly overwhelmed the doctor's words. Djuna caught in time the steering wheel as the car jolted against the shoulder of the road, kicking up a spray of gravel; she carefully steered back into her lane. Through the curve of her windshield, the sky was growing paler; the landscape took on texture and variation as the horizon began to redden.

"Do you think those memories will come back?" she'd asked the doctor yesterday. The buzzing in her ears had become a roar, so loud she wondered that he didn't hear it too. She'd had the sensation that her molecules might dissolve right there in the waiting room, go floating off like tiny colored balloons released into the atmosphere.

The neurologist had frowned, as if the question pained him. "I wish I could tell you for sure. The truth is, whether the origin of this amnesia is physical or psychological, I can't say for certain *that* she'll recover or *when*. It could happen tomorrow or next month or in five years or never."

As he'd stood awkwardly to leave, Djuna had recalled Suyuan's comment about how doctors needed to know the answers. She could read the frustration etched in lines around his mouth, his inability to meet his own expectations. It was not his fault, she decided, listening as his footsteps receded down the corridor. Her world was ending, the atoms reorganizing themselves at will, spinning too fast, out of control, but none of it was his fault.

She didn't know how long she'd sat there, clutching Dr. Hastings's crumpled handkerchief against her mouth. By the time she'd found the will to move, her leg had fallen asleep. Each step had sent fragments of pain shooting through the numbed leg, but she made her way to the elevators and down to the third floor, where she located a bank of pay phones.

If she'd thought about it, she wouldn't have dialed Evelyn's number. Evelyn did not see clients on Friday; there was no reason to expect her to be there. But Djuna had plunked in the coins and punched the numbers without thinking.

"Dr. Meyer," Evelyn had answered on the first ring.

This had brought Djuna up short; Evelyn never answered her phone. "It's Djuna," she'd sputtered. "But what are you doing there?"

The therapist's tone never wavered. "I stopped by the office to pick up a journal I wanted to read," she'd explained, then seamlessly shifted focus. "You sound upset. Did you want to talk to me, or shall I hang up and let you call back and leave a message?"

Djuna had launched into a recitation of the day's events. It surprised her how terse and stilted her voice sounded, stripped of emotion, as if she'd already used up the day's allotment of grief.

"I keep thinking it must be something I've done." Her words seemed forced from some hollow place in her throat.

"It's not your fault," Evelyn insisted. "It's not your fault, or her fault."

"I don't know," Djuna sighed and leaned her forehead against the metal wall of the phone booth. "Why else would I be the only one she can't remember?"

"You're not," Evelyn reminded her. "Remember, you said that when those young men came to see her, you know, her students—"

"Eric and Jorge."

"Yes, she didn't know *them*, and didn't you also tell me she couldn't recognize her therapist?"

It was all true, but Djuna could take no comfort in it. "Evelyn, I know *logically* that it's not personal, okay? But, goddamn it, it feels so fucking personal."

It had been Evelyn's suggestion to take the weekend off. "Take a break from the hospital, give yourself the chance to do something just for you," she'd urged. "Whether Bryn regains her memory or not, her recovery will likely take months, if not years. You're going to need to develop some other resources to sustain you over the long haul."

As sensible as Djuna knew that advice to be, it scared her to stay away from the hospital, even for one day. Some part of her stubbornly believed that if she could only find the right words, and say them at just the right time, she could pry open Bryn's locked brain like a sealed tomb.

The sign for her exit loomed in the near distance. Djuna took it, leaving the highway to veer onto a small road that would lead her away from the trailer parks and condos, the burger joints and shopping plazas that threatened to overrun the desert.

Her timing was off. The sky was already light blue, the sun glinting over the horizon, but no matter. She downed the last swig of coffee from the thermos, and followed the thin clouds, gauzy and drifting overhead.

It was nearly 8:00 when she pulled into the Joshua Tree National Monument. She paid the fee for day visitors and received a trail map from the park ranger. She parked the car in a dusty, gravel-filled lot, shut down the engine, and stepped outside. Djuna yawned and stretched, bending from the waist, letting the sleepless night and the long car trip drain from her muscles.

A breeze stirred the air, but the temperature was climbing with the sun's ascent. In her mind she heard Bryn's admonition, *Don't forget to put on sunscreen,* and obediently did so, spreading the greasy cream over her nose and arms, her neck, the skin of her legs left bare by her shorts. She pulled a knapsack from the trunk and packed it with a large bottle of water, two oranges, a sandwich bag full of trail mix, four rolls of film, a tripod, and the tube of sunscreen. Once she'd loaded the knapsack over her shoulders, she hung her camera from a strap around her neck. The addition of a baseball cap and dark sunglasses completed her outfit. She then locked the car and headed for the trail.

At this time of year, the desert was beautiful, with the earliest wild-flowers just beginning to bloom. Emily, blessed with an encyclopedic memory, would have been able to identify most of them, but Djuna could never hold that information in her brain. Still, she looked for the curl of petals amidst the gray-green foliage, a glimpse of yellow or violet or red.

After she'd walked for about forty minutes, she left the trail and headed for a cluster of Joshua trees, just beginning to flower this early in the season. She was looking for a place she and Bryn had scouted a few years ago; Djuna thought she recalled a clump of trees that looked like this. Bryn had wanted to find a place far from the trail, where the two of them could make love under the sky without the risk of discovery. It had taken all of Bryn's considerable powers of persuasion to get Djuna to discard her clothes; Djuna was by nature exceedingly modest, and not at all given to public display.

She could remember, though, the feeling of the sun on their naked bodies, the slick salt-sweat that had covered Bryn's reddening skin as she'd moaned for Djuna's fingers inside her, the way their cries sounded wild in the desert air, echoing off the face of the mountains. "I hope God was watching," was what Bryn had crooned into Djuna's ear after they'd both come, her voice half defiant and half worshipful. Djuna could almost feel again the sweet breath passing over her ear.

Tears began to dot the inside of the lenses of her sunglasses and carve a path through the dust that had settled on her cheeks. Evelyn had encouraged her to get away from Bryn for a while, but she might as well suggest Djuna cut the heart out of her own chest. The desert reminded her of Bryn, the light caress of breeze was her lover's touch, the sky, the sun, there was nothing not infused with Bryn's essence.

A lizard scuttled across her shadow and sped into the brush. Djuna slumped onto the dirt and let herself wail. She unleashed the camera from her neck and dropped the pack from her shoulders. Sobs escaped her throat like hiccups, blending with the call of the roadrunners, reverberating in the dry blue air.

She hoped God was listening.

33.

Vera

Vera sat in the empty hospital room, staring through the window as rain poured from the dense gray sky. It had been storming since Saturday night, the first rain in the nearly seven weeks she'd been here, the first deviation from the preternatural sunshine. The shift in weather seemed to alter the very nature of the city, to dim its flash and glitter, reduce the carefully cultivated glamour to something humbler, more human. On the street below, cars took more care to negotiate the water-slicked pavement, and pedestrians hunched their shoulders beneath umbrellas as they hurried for shelter. From this window Vera could see hills that were achingly green, as if something had come newly alive, with all the pain and promise that entailed.

Even as she observed the hills, the roiling clouds, the driving sheets of water, Vera was listening for the odd, three-footed rhythm, *thump-clack-clack*, of her daughter as she slowly made her way, with the help of a walker, along the corridor. For the last six days, Brenda had taken this halting journey down the hallway, each time a little farther. Her physical therapist was impressed with Brenda's progress, but it pained Vera to witness her daughter's slow, clumping step. At those times she had to remind herself to be grateful to God that Brenda was alive to walk at all.

Vera wondered whether Djuna was able to feel gratitude for Brenda's survival. Although Brenda was improving in many areas, her memory had not returned. And there was no use trying to fill in the five-year gap in her recollection; whatever Brenda could not remember, she was unwilling to accept. She had turned away her students and more recent friends, even her therapist, as inexorably as she'd rejected Djuna.

If Vera had once felt competitive with Djuna for Brenda's affections, she took no pleasure now in having won this rivalry. Every time she saw Djuna's face sag with disappointment, each time Brenda rebuffed her efforts at connection, Vera's heart was wrenched. She knew full well how devastated she would be were the situation reversed.

Now she turned her back to the downpour outside to study the room in which she had spent so many hours, the room in which her daughter had lain for weeks in a dreamless sleep, only to rise again. A room they were soon to vacate. The hospital was going to discharge Brenda on Wednesday.

Dr. Hastings had told them on Friday, taking herself and Djuna into the hallway to make the announcement. It had come as a shock. Vera supposed it had been foolish to assume that things could just go on as they had been, foolish but comforting. Despite the difficulties, the last few weeks in the hospital had offered a kind of routine, some small sense of being rooted in present time. Now the ground once more threatened to dissolve beneath them; the future loomed with menacing uncertainty.

Dr. Hastings was recommending that Brenda be placed in a rehabilitation facility in Tustin, a forty-five–minute drive from L.A. As an inpatient, she would continue to receive physical, occupational, and speech therapy, as well as psychological counseling, if they wished. He had, he assured Djuna, already established that Suyuan would be a part of Brenda's rehabilitation team.

This made sense to Vera; she had faith in the neurologist and trusted his recommendations. She'd been caught off guard when Djuna asked, "What if . . . I mean, couldn't she go to Tustin as an outpatient, and . . . uh . . . come *home?* I mean, wouldn't it be better for her to be in her own environment?"

The doctor fielded the inquiry with sensitivity; he seemed to understand all that was invested in the question. "I do see that as an option down the road," he confirmed, "but right now she's still in need of skilled, round-the-clock care."

"Couldn't we bring somebody in to do that?" Djuna persisted. "How is she supposed to remember her life if she's kept away from it?"

"My biggest concern," Dr. Hastings responded evenly, "is that Bryn receives all the care she needs to facilitate her recovery. At this critical stage, she's remapping her neurological pathways. If we neglect some aspect of her development now, we may not have another chance."

Djuna hadn't been able to let go of her resistance. "Well, why can't she see her own therapist? I mean, for psychological counseling."

The doctor had appeared to grow just a little impatient. "My understanding is that she doesn't remember her psychotherapist and has refused to see her."

"We could just as easily introduce her therapist as a new doctor, since if we brought in somebody new we'd have to do that anyway," Djuna's voice had grown louder, its pitch more shrill. "I can't understand why it doesn't seem to matter to you that Bryn has continuity. Yeah, I want to see her able to function again, of course, but I want her to function as the woman she was before the accident!"

Dr. Hastings had frowned. "Djuna, we all want that, but there's just no guarantee. We're still learning about the interplay of forces—genetic, environmental, psychological—that determine what we think of as the 'self.'"

He'd put a hand on Djuna's shoulder then. "I don't know how much Bryn will be like she was before. But I do know there are ways to help her relearn to walk, to speak, to write. I want to make sure we do those things that we know are effective, and that we do them now."

Before he turned to go, he'd added, "I'll check with their administrator about Bryn's therapist. If she's got the proper certification and she's willing to drive to Tustin, I don't see any problem with that."

The next day, Vera had explained to Brenda what was going to happen, omitting Djuna's alternate plan. But Brenda had her own opinion. Bored with her confinement, restless, she had no interest in going to another hospital. What she wanted was to go home with Vera, back to Detroit. "You're mother," she'd kept insisting. "Be with you."

It startled Vera. How many years had it been since Brenda had expressed a wish to be near her; how long since she'd looked into her mother's face with total expectancy and trust? Vera could recall the radiance of that gaze from when her daughter was a little girl. Vera had come to believe that light was forever lost to her, like a star burned out of the sky. Seeing it glimmer once more in her daughter's eyes was as unnerving as it was seductive.

Dr. Hastings was right, of course; it would not be in Brenda's best interest to risk such a transfer. A move of that nature was bound to be stressful, and not only on the body. She couldn't run the risk that her daughter might lose the ground she had worked so hard to gain. Vera understood all this, yet part of her felt helpless in the face of Brenda's adamant plea: "Mama, take me home."

She hadn't mentioned Brenda's request to Djuna; she saw no point in upsetting her further. Vera had spent enough time with Djuna to imagine her response, the chin jutting defensively, eyes lit as if by fire, the combative set of her shoulders. The last thing Vera wanted was to provoke a power struggle with Djuna; nothing good would come from that.

Too, she was confused about which of them had the authority to make decisions about Brenda now. Djuna still held the power of attorney, but might Brenda be considered competent to make her own determination?

Complicating everything was Brenda's memory loss. Over the weekend she'd asked Vera to "tell that strange woman"—meaning Djuna—"to stop bothering me." If asked today, she would certainly choose Vera as her proxy, but could her current state of mind be said to reflect her true wishes? If how she was before the accident was different than how she was now, which could be considered the "real" Brenda?

It made Vera's head hurt to think about it. She'd only gone through high school; how was she supposed to know about all this? They should just agree to do what the doctor was recommending, which was probably the best for Brenda anyway.

Still, she'd raised with Everett the possibility of her daughter coming home to stay when she'd called him last night, Sunday, when the rates were low. He was increasingly cranky and short with her when she spoke to him. Asked whether he missed her, he would only grumble, "It's hard to do everything here by myself."

She'd broached the matter tentatively, "Wouldn't it be something if. . . ." He'd been predictably negative. Didn't Vera suppose she was too old to take on such a big responsibility? How could they manage in their small townhouse, with no bedroom on the ground floor? And how the heck did she think they could afford it?

And what, really, Vera asked herself, did she imagine? That the three of them could re-form themselves into a family? *"I have split the web of family. . . ."* Her daughter had written that. How long would it take until she felt that way again?

It was crazy, a pipe dream; every practicality weighed against it.

The doctor opposed it; Djuna would never forgive her; Everett would never allow it. She had to get a hold of herself, be firm, *be realistic,* as Everett had said.

It was only the look in Brenda's eyes, open as sunlight, as faith. It was only knowing how that look would turn, disappointment flooding her eyes, the sun melting into a lake at dusk, swallowed and drowned. This look, too, Vera remembered from her daughter's childhood, the look of trust betrayed, and then the one that followed it: the face hardening, closing in on itself like a door slammed shut forever. Vera had never dreamed she'd be given another chance with Brenda. How could she throw it away?

Once, perhaps ten years ago, Brenda had complained that Vera had chosen Chet over her. "You stayed with him, Mom, even when I begged you not to," she'd accused.

Vera had explained that she'd thought she was making the best choice for both of them. "I'd already been a single mom once, after Carl left. I knew what it was like to worry all the time, to not be able to afford anything. I didn't want to do that to you again."

Brenda's mouth had curled bitterly. "We should have just taken our chances, Mom. We would have been okay."

Maybe she should just take a chance, Vera thought, and do what her daughter was asking her to do.

Along the hall Vera could hear the *thump-clack-clack* of her daughter's return. Preceded by the legs of the metal walker, Brenda clomped into the room. It was always a shock to see her at first, her hair now entirely silver; Vera never expected it. Her daughter's face was red with effort, her T-shirt soaked in sweat. When she reached the bed, she collapsed onto it in genuine exhaustion; Vera caught the walker and moved it against the wall. She helped Brenda to resettle in the bed.

"You were gone for a long time, huh?" she said as she plumped the pillow behind her daughter's head. "Did you make it all the way around the floor? I'm really proud of you; you're doing so well."

"Thirsty," Brenda ordered, her breath still coming in shallow gasps. She waited for her mother to supply some water, but Dr. Hastings had cautioned Vera that it was important to let Brenda do things for herself.

"There's your cup," Vera pointed to the tray, then watched as Brenda struggled upright and fumbled to bring the container to her lips.

She drank in greedy gulps, water dribbling down her chin; it puddled in dark splotches on the bib of her T-shirt. It took three attempts to land the cup back on the bedside tray. These tasks accomplished, Brenda fell back onto the pillow. "I'm all smashed," she said.

"Are you tired, honey?" Vera asked. "Do you want a little nap?"

"Not to sleep," her daughter scowled. "Just my bones."

"Okay, then, just rest," Vera soothed, as she'd done when Brenda was a kid and couldn't get to sleep.

"Story?" Brenda asked, her eyes hopeful. She wanted Vera to read to her.

"How about if I get a book, and you can practice reading," Vera suggested carefully. Dr. Hastings had urged her to persuade Brenda to read as much as possible. "You can tell me a story."

Brenda sighed and kicked one foot against the mattress, but she did not refuse outright, so Vera fetched a book from the closet shelf and handed it to her daughter. It was *Andersen's Fairy Tales,* a book Brenda had kept from childhood, and one of several Vera had plucked from the shelves in her daughter's living room. Brenda leafed through its pages with a listless disinterest, then stopped when she came to a particular story.

"This one," she declared, and jabbed at the page with her index finger extended. Vera perched on the side of the bed, close enough to be able to prompt if her daughter failed to recognize a word.

"The Snow Queen," Brenda read, forming each word with great care, as if the syllables were unfamiliar on her tongue.

"You used to love that story," Vera reminded her. "Do you remember, you'd ask grandma to read it over and over until her voice was hoarse."

For a moment, her daughter's face was blank as an empty plate, then a smile cracked its surface. "Grandma!" she chirped, victorious. "I remember. She used to sing pansies."

Vera wasn't sure what that meant, but it frustrated Brenda when she wasn't understood, so Vera tried to direct her attention back to the book. "Go on," she urged.

Brenda resumed her recitation, squinting at the page in the manner of the nearsighted. "First story," she narrated, "Which Treats of the Mirror and Fragments." She seemed to have little trouble recognizing the words, but she read them in such a halting, uninflected style that it was impossible to know whether or not she grasped their meaning. Vera couldn't help mourn, thinking of how beautiful her daughter's speech had been before the accident, its clear and vivid intonations.

Although she recalled that Brenda loved this story, Vera did not remember the plot. She wasn't sure she'd ever read it before. She gazed through the window at the rain, lulled by the tuneless drone of her daughter's voice. She half listened to the tale of Gerta and Kay, children who loved each other. She almost missed the part where Kay got the splinter in his eye that froze his heart, and the next thing Vera knew, he was being carried away by the Snow Queen to her icy kingdom.

Much of the story was taken up with Gerta's search to find her lost love, and Vera drifted in and out of it. Time seemed to swim before her, no longer static with regular divisions of minutes and years, irretrievably separate, but fluid now, a continuous river. Memories flooded her, out of sequence, unrelenting. With her daughter's monotone encircling her ears, Vera once more studied the wall of photographs in a bright yellow room; at the same time she searched, with Chet, the nooks and crannies of a cramped rented house, trying to find her daughter's hiding place. She talked with Lowell over good wine in a dark restaurant while Brenda, twenty, boarded a plane for California, not looking back to wave good-bye. She watched Djuna pace back and forth in the hospital room as three-year-old Brenda clung to her grandmother's lap, wailing in protest as Vera tried to take her.

The swell and flow of time surrounded Vera, swirled into Brenda's dogged recital, the story of Kay's rescue from his frozen imprisonment. It was Gerta who never lost faith, even as she journeyed to the coldest regions of the world. And when she found Kay, he did not remember her.

"Stop crying," Brenda commanded suddenly, her voice puzzled and scared.

Until her daughter spoke, Vera hadn't realized she was weeping. "I will," she promised, wiping at her eyes. "See? It's done." She smiled in reassurance.

"It's not so sad," Brenda whispered, abandoning the book, the story unfinished, by her side. Her lids were heavy with the day's exertions; in moments she had drifted into sleep.

Vera lifted the book from the mattress and stayed seated on the edge of the bed, hugging the volume to her chest. Opening the front cover, she saw Brenda's name scrawled in crayon, an entry made over thirty years ago. With one finger, she traced its clumsy cursive.

She stood abruptly then and leaned across the bed to kiss her daughter's cheek. Brenda stirred and shifted, but did not awaken. Vera leaned closer to her ear, which smelled of soap and sweat.

"I'm sorry, baby, but you can't go home with me. You worked all your life to get here, and I can't take you away." The words seemed to have sharp edges that sliced the cords of her throat but she could not hold them back.

"I know you're lost now, my little girl, but I promise you, someone's looking for you. And she'll find you, honey, she won't give up. She'll find you."

34.

Bryn

Wires loop to nowhere, spark and fizzle. When you cut wires under the hood, the car won't go. Poor dead brain, old lump of meat. Legs don't obey, fingers won't help, tongue can't . . .

I'm not who I used to be. Someone's face fills the mirror, but I don't know her. I trace her features like lines on a map, but it's not a country I have ever visited, and no markings point the way home.

Music is a rope I cling to. Notes dance across broken wires, rhythm spirals and connects. Music speaks to the part of my brain that didn't get hammered; every tone, each beat, tells a story to my cells.

I've seen pictures of the person I used to be. They bring them to me. I squint and stare, try to read the image for its definition, but there's only an echo of familiarity, the ghost of a shadow, a stirring of breath. "Who is this she?" I want to know. Someone else fills the mirror now. Her hair is metal, her eyes look strange. I don't know if I like her.

There is a garden here, and they let me walk outside, feel the sun on my skin. I can pluck an iris, its thin, soft petals like the flesh of old women. I pick a lemon from the tree and hold that bright globe in my hands; it smells sweet and sharp, like a flower that could cut you. I listen to the music of birds and am certain they are telling stories. I wish I understood their language.

They tell me I was full of stories. Somehow I've lost them. Where did they go? Are they flying loose, birds lost from the flock? Were they dropped like shiny coins from a pocket? Maybe someone picked them up, took my stories for their own. Maybe there's someone out there in the world, spending my stories like loose change.

I have a watch with a big, big face, and big, big numbers. One, two, seven, nine. The hands spin fast or slow; time makes no sense. One minute can stretch until it holds the history of life, and yet it seems no more than a minute that I've been alive. I was a child once, I guess. They tell me I am forty years old. How many minutes are in forty years?

They tell me there are things I don't remember. What things? Are they stories? Are they lemons? Are they stars? If I don't remember them, who does? Is it a secret that everyone knows but me? Does that mean they know me better than I know myself? Or is it someone else they know, with her forgotten lemons, someone who's nothing like me?

Suyuan tells me not to worry all these questions. She tells me it's okay to drift like a boat on the open sea, no rudder, no sail. She tells me to trust the current, let the water carry me home.

There's a shrink who comes to see me, too. She has a good face. She says she knew me before. I tell her, "Don't be so sure."

When she asks how I feel, I shrug and say, "Something was full. Now it's empty. Stories gone, years gone. I sag like a paper sack."

My mother is gone. She's on another map now, Detroit. I cried like a baby when she left. Then I remembered how I always felt she was gone.

Lowell is gone too; she never comes to see me.

Suyuan comes, Emily comes. It's hard with Emily. She's got a big engine, she drives fast. All the wires spiral and hum. She goes places I can't follow; I watch her taillights in the distance, taste exhaust.

There's someone else. The woman with hair like a spiky crown. Her eyes as dark as a nighttime lake, sad as though someone had drowned there. She comes every day. She brought me a pretty dress, yellow roses in a green vase. She brought me music.

She says her name is June. That's the month when summer begins. She comes every day. At first it bothered me, the way she stares at me, like she's lost something and thinks I might know where to find it. But I've grown to like her face. It's honest. I can read it like a map.

She brought me a photograph of a desert scape to hang on the wall. It looks so pretty I want to go there. In the foreground is a clump of Joshua trees, ragged and gnarled as old men. In the background, mountains barricade the horizon. In the middle, there's a blur, something almost human, perhaps female, not yet defined. She seems to be rising from the desert floor, emerging from the dust that blows in the air. Shapeless, formless, all suggestion and possibility.

About the Author

Terry Wolverton is the author of *Black Slip*, a collection of poetry published by Clothespin Fever Press, which was nominated for a Lambda Book Award in 1993. Her fiction, poetry, essays and drama have been published in periodicals internationally—including *Glimmer Train Stories, Zyzzyva*, and *The Jacaranda Review*—and widely anthologized.

She has also edited several successful compilations, including *Blood Whispers: L.A. Writers on AIDS, Volumes 1* and *2* (Silverton Books, 1991 and 1994) and (with Robert Drake) *Indivisible: Short Fiction by West Coast Gay and Lesbian Writers* (Plume, 1991) and *His: Brilliant New Fiction by Gay Men* and *Hers: Brilliant New Fiction by Lesbians* (Faber and Faber, 1995).

She currently resides in Los Angeles with her partner, visual artist Susan Silton.